'By the Light of the Silvery Mo... caress, contemplate, kill, comp... collection of stories, drawn tog... birthday of Silver Moon Wom... addresses the silvery moon in myriad ways: romance, sci-fi, myth and magic, witty domestic dramas, and sly pointers about creativity are all here. The contributors are: Lisa Alther, Liza Cody, Merle Collins, Fiona Cooper, Zoë Fairbairns, Ellen Galford, Elizabeth Jolley, Shena Mackay, Sara Maitland, Moy McCrory, Suniti Namjoshi and Gillian Hanscombe, Sarah Schulman, Hanan al-Shaykh, and Lisa Tuttle – all writers who have found an enthusiastic audience in the shop over its luminous decade.

Ruth Petrie, who has edited this collection, is Virago's Senior Editorial Director.

By the Light of the Silvery Moon

SHORT STORIES
TO CELEBRATE THE 10TH
BIRTHDAY OF SILVER MOON
WOMEN'S BOOKSHOP

EDITED BY RUTH PETRIE

Published by VIRAGO PRESS Limited 1994
42–43 Gloucester Crescent, London NW1 7PD

Printed and bound in Great Britain by
Cox & Wyman Ltd, Reading, Berkshire

Contents

PREFACE   Sue Butterworth and Jane Cholmeley   vii

THE SILVER APPLES OF THE MOON
  Elizabeth Jolley   1

LANTERNS   Moy McCrory   11

MOONWALK   Ellen Galford   19

MANSKIN, WOMANSKIN   Lisa Tuttle   35

CAN'T HELP IT   Sarah Schulman   51

SILVER MOON BAY   Lisa Alther   61

THE LADIES ARE UPSTAIRS   Merle Collins   77

SIREN SONG Sara Maitland   83

LOVE FINDS SHIRLEY TEMPEST   Fiona Cooper   95

CHALK MOTHER   Liza Cody   109

TROUSER LADIES   Shena Mackay   117

HEARTSEASE   Hanan al-Shaykh   129

HEY DIDDLE DIDDLE!
  Gillian Hanscombe & Suniti Namjoshi   145

BY THE LIGHT OF THE SILVERY MOON
  Zoë Fairbairns   157

Notes on Contributors   165

Preface

THIS COLLECTION of short stories celebrates the tenth birthday of Silver Moon Women's Boookshop. It also celebrates the hard work and good humour of the many women who have worked here.

We first thought of opening a feminist bookshop in the centre of London over twelve years ago – we wanted women's books and issues to be on the high street where they could not be ignored and marginalised. The shop opened on the original site at 68 Charing Cross Road on 31st May, 1984 with 850 square feet. That first day we took £250 and were so excited we forgot to re-order any books.

Ten years on we have expanded and now stretch from 64–68 Charing Cross Road, the busiest bookselling road in the world. We are now Britain's only women's bookshop and the largest in Europe. All this has been achieved through the constant support and encouragement of our customers, both here and abroad. Thank you all.

We have been privileged to meet many authors. They, and the other writers whose books we stock, have inspired us, comforted and confronted us. Women's writing has brought us joy and that rare gift of combining entertainment and strength.

Many publishers and suppliers have worked with us during the years but we are particularly delighted that the co-operation and friendship we have enjoyed with Virago are celebrated in this marvellous anthology. Many of the authors collected here have visited the shop to read in the last decade and, as always, we are grateful for their skill and time.

Over the last ten years we have sold women the books they want, and in return they have given us the priceless gift of allowing us to earn a living doing what we love most. Knowledge is power. We hope that by providing a space for women's ideas we have helped fuel our debates, sharpened our analysis and made a real contribution to breaking through discrimination and advancing the status of all women. At the same time we are glad to have brought income and sustenance to women writers.

Finally, as we move towards the millenium, Silver Moon Women's Bookshop stands as a reminder that dreams really do come true.

Sue Butterworth and Jane Cholmeley
London, February, 1994

The Silver Apples of the Moon

ELIZABETH JOLLEY

BERYL. WHAT do you mean, *the golden apples of the sun, the silver apples of the moon*? It's not like you, this isn't. Are you unwell? Have you been to the doctor? What does Hugh think? Worry! I've never been so worried. Since the passing of dear Robbo I've had no one to talk things out with. I simply can't say, as I used to, Robbo what the hell's Beryl on about this time...

Beryl. You say this man never speaks. You say he simply sits there not speaking and not looking at you, simply sits there in your house not even speaking to you or looking at you. For hours on end, you say, he does this.

How old is this man and what is his name? *He never speaks* you say. I can't take it like this, that you have him there the way you do. Last winter when you wrote and said, 'We have this man coming to sleep here he comes about seven or eight and we put the folding bed in the lounge and he gets up about half past five because he's supposed to leave early ...' I couldn't take it then and I can't take it now. How long is it now? I simply cannot picture you and Hugh doing something like this.

This man has a bath you say; you are *supposed* to let him have a *bath* and one meal either at night or in the morning? Who decides *that* I'd like to know? And who pays for the hot water and the food? How can you and Hugh, the both of you *do* this. Not that I think it's wrong or anything. But I mean, having a perfect stranger coming into the house to *sleep*. I *mean*! You could be stabbed. The both of you could be robbed and stabbed and worse in your beds. I know it's a kind action to *take in* someone who hasn't any home but surely it's meant to be only temporary. The Homeless Person is not meant to go on coming and is definitely not meant to stay all day and surely he should let you know when he's coming. He surely can't simply turn up when it suits him. What about your own arrangements? What happens if you have visitors in the lounge? You say you never have anyone visit you now and, you say, after being bossy all the summer saying everything you do – hedges, lawns, edges, pruning, the hedges and the gutters – is all wrong, he goes off and doesn't help with anything. How could you let this person do this? Why doesn't Hugh talk to him and tell him it's not on? Surely Hughie could give him the *word*.

If Hugh should go, you know what I mean, if Hugh should *pass on* I hope he won't of course but he has got fifteen years head start; if he should go *before* you – and this person is living in your house, as he seems to think he is, he might well claim you know, what they call it, a *de facto* and then what about the will and your assets? Where will *you* be, Beryl, if this person stays on and claims half of everything? You must think about the odds. I know it's back to winter and it's cold and you can't bring yourself to tell him he must go. And I can understand that you're *drawn* because this man is poetic and loves music, classical music, you say; I should perhaps point out that *The Four Seasons* is hardly more than pop these days, Vivaldi has certainly caught on. I know that Hugh has no ear and he wouldn't have a clue where poetry's concerned. Yeats

2

wouldn't mean a thing to Hughie. I'd go on to say, Beryl, that most people these days wouldn't have a clue as to Yeats and I'll say straight out that your visitor wouldn't last long in *this* house with his *glimmering girl with apple blossom in her hair* and his *kissings of the lips* and walking *among long dappled grass*, and who'd want to be picking gold and silver apples? Be real Beryl. Believe you me, he, that man, he'll be having a girl to sleep over before you know it and I can tell you girls mess up a house something terrible with their bits of wet underwear draped all over the place and hair in the bathroom basin and sure enough she'll want to cook. She'll be through your deep freeze and ruining your stainless steel before you can turn round. You'll never have your own kitchen when you want it. I tell you Beryl! People!

I'm warning you Beryl. You can't say I didn't warn you that time Sylvie had someone sleep over and Hughie looked out the window in the morning. I'll never forget you telling me that he raised the roof when he saw that boy's car parked on the lawn.

Is he still here, he wanted to know, if he's still here what does he think he's doing? And you told him that – it's all right Hughie, he's sleeping over that's all . . .

Sleeping over! Hughie couldn't take it, could he? Sleeping over, he took it like a dog takes a bone, you told me, he wouldn't drop it. Not in my house he kept on, you said, and then Hughie wanted to know why this boy had slept over, he wanted to know what was wrong with the back of the car, the back seat of the car . . .

I warned you Beryl you can't say I didn't warn you then. I said, *you allow one you'll get them all* like bees round a honey pot. As I remember – if I'm wrong . . . I tell a lie – but as I remember that young man brought his things to your place. You had him there *weeks*. He only left when the police caught up with him and fetched him away. Beryl, if you face the truth that's how you lost Sylvie. If you'd spoken up that first time, if

3

you'd said, *not in my house Sylvie*, you'd never have lost her the way you have and she'd be nicely married. (I used to picture her wedding right from when she could just walk – the pretty little girl!) *Nicely married*, I say, and living in a house of her own, just around the corner from you, all settled with a nice husband and a couple of little kiddies, her own little family. As it is you don't even know where she is.

Your trouble, Beryl, has always been that you couldn't speak up and now you can't tell this person he can't come to your place any more. You can't speak up Beryl and neither can Hughie. Raise the roof, he can do that all right, but it's only you he's raising the roof at and what's the point of raising the roof at your own wife? I ask you!

I know you say you can't sleep knowing the HP is out in the cold, well, just you listen to me for a change: for every homeless person sleeping in someone's lounge room there's a dozen sleeping in the park or under the station bridge, so just what good do you think you're doing?

You say yourself he's found lodgings, he's got a room paid a month in advance, you say. He's wasting his money, isn't he, if he doesn't move into this other room? Now you listen to me Beryl: now that he's got this place to go to you should take a firm stand. A phone not answered stops ringing, you know this as well as I do. I just can't understand why he wants to be in your house if he just sits there, as you say he does, *in a mood* and not speaking to you or to Hughie. It's not right Beryl, you can't have him brooding there like that and you not knowing what he's brooding about. You must tell him straight that it's not on, not any more. Tell him you've been to the doctor and you're not well. Tell him Hugh's gone mad. Tell him you've got to go to hospital, tell him you've got to have an operation, a woman's operation.

Beryl. I'm not surprised, not surprised at all that the both of you were took with food poisoning. You don't have to tell me what it was *I can tell*. You should never ever have ate all that expensive rubbish, not any of it, specially not the duck and orange patty, even if there was brandy in it. Brandy only adds heat to food poisoning. You should've known that. I know you were afraid of hurting your person's pride but people shouldn't give presents they can't afford, to people they hardly know. It's not manners, is it, to do this? You must keep in mind he was nearly the death of poor Hughie, let alone yourself. I won't remind you that it was your own fault you getting yourself into this position in the first place.

Who does this man think he is spending money he hasn't got on cold cuts of rare beef (Hughie could *never* eat red beef), turkey, chicken *and* ham, smoked salmon and those dreadful cheeses full of diseases and then the flowers, all those frozen orchids? Knowing you and Hughie most of it went straight in the bin. Hughie was always a plain eater, even as a little boy he'd go for steak and chips, never touched any vegetable except for peas. He'd never touch gravy, not a drop I've seen him scrape gravy off his steak. But you should know this.

Throw it away Beryl, the whole lot if you haven't already done so. And don't forget flowers give Hughie a headache...

Beryl. What do you mean? *The golden apples of the sun, the silver apples of the moon*. It's not like you Beryl. Well not like you as you used to be. Are you poorly Beryl? Have you been to the doctor? You can tell me Beryl. You can tell me *anything*, you know that. And what's all this about a piano and a cello? This time you've got me really worried. This man. What's all this about him getting a *friend* for you? You've got Hughie and, though I'm his sister and shouldn't say it as does, you couldn't do better than Hughie, solid as a rock as they say and safe as houses, you don't need anyone else, Beryl, especially someone got for you by this *person*. You should listen to me, Beryl, this man's taking you over. Have you spoken about it to Hughie? One thing I'm certain of you'll never get a nasty infection from Hughie, always lived a clean and decent life Hughie has. I should know having brought him up ever since Mum went. But who knows what you'll get from the company this person keeps. And another thing, it appears the *friend* is a *woman*. Believe you me, Beryl, it might be amusing for you, as you say, to have this visitor rabbitting on about a woman friend for you but it's not *natural* Beryl, I mean the way he's thought it all out, how she would look at you with *serious tenderness* and that it is a fact that her eyes make up for lack of beauty in the nose and the chin and for the haggard look which distinguishes her from other women. Well, we all *know* what makes a woman look like that even though your HP explains it away as painful and secret experience. And Beryl how can he presume to tell you what to wear? You are touched, you say, when he describes you and this so-called lady friend being mysterious and somewhat shabby in your drapery and wearing your hair looped under forward dipping hats, and, I can hardly bring myself to think about this next thing, this *intimacy*, a shared responsibility, he says, you would tell each other if your slips were showing and you would dust off each other's excess talc. This is ludicrous Beryl, you actually let him say these things to you when he's not brooding and silent. He'll come up with worse Beryl, don't ever say I didn't warn you.

It might be amusing Beryl to talk about drapery. It might be *amusing* Beryl but he's paving the way for *something*. I can only warn you and you will appreciate my being twelve thousand miles away doesn't make it any easier. What does Hughie say to all this talk about this woman's voice being like a piano and cello sonata? I ask you how can a human voice be like that? I know he says *tremulous* and *sustained, pleading* and *reassuring*. Beryl, he's over the top. You must see that.

And then there's this outing he's supposed to have planned for you on a river boat you say, with this woman, a shared experience during which a glance or an arching of the eyebrows *can speak so much*. You will visit a cathedral and see a lantern, the only one of its kind in England, ecclesiastical, high up in the roof, *wonderfully light* and *awesome*. You will float in the boat between grass banks where a crested grebe will stand not moving at the water's edge and the boat will pass silently on between two long fields of flax in deep blue flower. And on this boat apparently, according to your *person*, you will sit watching four women passing one piece of knitting from one to another, during the pauses at the lock gates – each one taking a turn – unrolling the wool a little more with the knitting needles in constant movement.

Beryl. Listen to me. There's nothing you don't know about knitting. You don't need to share knitting with anyone. Which reminds me, I've got this ducky cable stitch pattern, the very thing for a pullover for Hughie. I'll send it. There! Get me on knitting and I'm away off the rails . . .

All I can say, Beryl, about this proposed outing is that I simply am not able to see you going off like that. My memory of English rivers is that it's always raining on them and they are very dull with no house or shop or cinema within reach, miles from the nearest bus or train and, if there *are* any *people*, they're old men sitting hunched up under their oilskins trying to catch fish in these damp places all overhung with dripping wet trees and only a few depressed cows for company. These old men they sit like that for hours.

Beryl I don't see that this *person* can invent a friend or an outing for you. What cheek to suggest that you need either when you've got Hughie alive and kicking. Where would Hughie fit in on this river boat with the lady friend and her eyes and her eyebrows? He wouldn't know where to put himself being shy with the ladies. He's always been comfortable with *you* Beryl as you well know.

'I'm very comfortable with Beryl. Beryl and me we're very comfortable.' If I've heard him say it once I've heard it a thousand times. You two simply do not need anyone else. Hasn't the thought ever occurred to either of you? You're two peas in a pod you are. That's it Beryl. Two peas in a pod. Snug as two bugs in a rug, as the saying goes. I ask myself this question Beryl: how much longer can you two be expected to put up with this intrusion? For intrusion it is. I know this person *seems* to be a breath of air, a poem, a musical interlude in your life, and I can see that he proposes to enliven your incredibly dull and, dare I say, useless existence with the company of a lady friend and an outing and his intention – his promise if you like – truly as he says, to bring you silver apples from the moon. Here I must warn you, Beryl, he is not talking money with these apples. They are probably worthless, wrapped in foil to disguise their poor quality, you know the way they do the mandarin oranges at Christmas.

These, shall I say, spurious gifts, if they can be called gifts, are considered by him to be a fair return for filling your lounge room with himself and his rain soaked shoes and clothes at all hours of the day and night. In his eyes these so called gifts compensate for the sheer discomfort caused by his presence in your comfy little nest. A nest which, you must remember, is the result of your faithful and regular good natured habit towards each other. A nest which can be described with complete truth as a love nest for two. Beryl, if you are the tiniest bit wise, you will see this nest as *threatened* and you will see the advantage of my offering this *person* the use of my centrally heated conservatory for drying off his wet clothes. In addition I am prepared, at great sacrifice of my personal space and freedom, which, as you know, I cherish, to offer him and the lady in question my own fun loving, try anything once, wealthy widowhood and the half of a healthy double bed. Perhaps you could tell him he can leave his silver apples on the moon. And tell him I'll fly him, *them*, direct, First Class ... And Beryl look sharp! I don't know how to say this, but my *impatience is so fretted* I could hang myself ...

Beryl. Yes of course I know I was misquoting Samuel Johnson. *You* don't need to tell *me*.

* * *

What's all this about me being too late? Beryl what on earth's going on? What do you mean? I am never late and have never ever been too late for anything. All my life I've never missed out on anything. You *know* this Beryl. And what's all this;

> How sweet the moonlight sleeps upon the bank
> Here will we sit, and let the sounds of music
> creep in our ears.

Beryl, I don't know of any bank near your place, Beryl. You say it's Shakespeare, I didn't know you knew him. Beryl, you've never ever mentioned Shakespeare in all the years. And Beryl you say the new Friend, the Lady Friend has the legs of an athlete half her age and that she makes certain requests, *demands*, is the word you use. You say you and Hughie have traded your bed, that *nice bed* (with the mahogany trim) for a new Queen Size *oval*, you say. Beryl, I don't want to hear about the mirrors. I will just say this Beryl, it's not natural to walk on anyone's stomach.

Beryl, you realise don't you you'll have to spend a fortune on new bed sheets, pillow slips to say nothing of a Queen Doona ... then there's the new mattress cover, the new electric blanket, the moved bed lamps ... I could go on ... the bedside tables ...

Beryl, and another thing, I've read that this walking on stomachs is the custom among certain tribes dwelling in the great deserts of the world but for them it is purely a remedy for constipation.

Lanterns

MOY McCRORY

IT'S NOT possible to remember the
way I do sometimes, like I can almost feel things. I think
I've forgotten everything, and then next minute I could put
my hand out and touch something that vanished ten years
ago – wallop. I probably have a defective gene that's left me
cursed with texture. When I think about the past I remember
surfaces. I feel things which were metal and angular, weeks
which felt spiky as if the days had blades stuck into them.
And softness, oddly. A street carved out of soot receding
like a tunnel. Thick, soft soot. If you touched the sides your
fingers would poke through into the darkness waiting just
beyond, but inside the tunnelled street was all crumbling velvet
like up the back of the chimney. The houses, where they'd still
to draw their curtains, caused glassy squares of light to cut
into it.

Windows felt hard, like the fruit spangles that I sucked,
slow, slow, until the middle wore thin as picture glass and
cracked open against the roof of my mouth. I'd push my
tongue through the hole until all that was left was the outer rim
of splintering sweet.

11

They'll be waiting like they always do. The prodigal returns. I said the days had blades stuck into them, some of them had been there so long they were buried over, hidden the way knives are, in soap or loaves of bread, and smuggled into prisons. Once I'd excavated the sharp metal hatred of those days I put it to good use and hacked my way out. I've never stopped escaping. Running. Like the first time I raced up through that long soft street in all that suffocating blackness. I didn't know where.

I hate all this. Hate it. The prodigal returns. Pretend to be OK. Life good to me. I am suffocating with duty, as the soot and softness of that street wraps around me again, fills my lungs, stops me breathing. The prodigal returns. Anniversary.

I hold a potato peeler in my hand. The bread knife has serrated edges as it lies on the chopping board in the kitchen. I watched her saw the top off the turnip. It is pushed to one side. It will go back in place, a lid for my lantern head, when the rest has been scooped out and the face cut through, then it will stop the wind snuffing out my candle.

She starts me off, digging inside the turnip. She leaves the rough white lumps on the wooden board, then switches to another tool, silvered metal, it takes out narrow white cores, which splay like a ghastly pianist and remind me of that game, dead-man's-finger.

Careful, careful. I dig into the white heart. Pull more fingers out. They claw the sides of the board. The turnip's flesh is fibrous. It rasps against the blade.

'Harder,' she tells me. I dig down. 'Use both hands.' I pull out plugs of turnip. As the inside hollows out, the vegetable walls appear slowly.

'Follow the curve of the turnip,' she says. 'Watch it! You'll go straight through the face.'

Inside the head the pulp is moist and shrinks back as I

push, using all my strength, the fibre liquefies. My hand is very small to handle a knife. She stands over me, watches. But she was always scared. Like she knew.

I sit by the window upstairs and listen. The distant rumble of cars, the sound of shoes as a woman clacks her way home, the dull glow from the Chinese take-away, sulphur lights in the high street. Some nights the moon seemed to balance itself right at the end of the street, hanging over the glassworks like a naked bulb where the workyard was covered with thousands of beadlike rod ends. Nights like this the moon would ripple over the glass waste and the loading shute was choked with jewels: yellow, opal, moonglassed.

I want to go to the moon. So badly, my mother promises. 'When they have rides we'll be among the first to go – OK? For a day trip. Now get out from under my feet.' And he's there suddenly, to explain how it isn't possible. But I'm excited by the imminence of the trip: I want maps of the stars so I can name the sights we'll pass, like going to the Lakes.

She blames herself. She blames herself. No one knew. 'I didn't know. How could I? He never spoke to me about things. You didn't in those days. Men and women just got on with it. He never told me nothing.' We gather for the anniversary. Strength in numbers. We still don't speak. These days.

He stands there, explaining how it's impossible with facts and figures. Later, when I am old enough to know that trips to the moon are out, Neil Armstrong walks on it. We watch it on satellite, not understanding.

'Aren't those spacemen brave Mam?'

'They are indeed. Going all that way alone.' She looks out the window at the pouring rain. 'And in this weather too.'

My father shakes his head. He'll explain how suddenly it is possible with facts and figures. As if this makes everything clear. She watches him, thinks he's trying to kid her. A neighbour says it's all propaganda, trick photographs in the newspaper, and all the street agrees the weather's gone berserk since they've been up there larking about. He shakes his head again at how simple we are. But for people like him who can explain everything with figures, numbers, science, where would the rest of us be? Solidly he proves the presence of God with watertight logic we'd be crazy to pit our wits against.

My texture for God was always of plastic, and of something tight, long before I discovered sex, before I knew the look of condoms. There's a moment I always think of, just after, if someone's used one, and I try to imagine what it feels like, with this thing, when it still clings, before the penis shrinks back. That moment, before it's slipped off, rolled up and flushed away. That moment of clinging uselessness.

'Don't watch me,' my lovers say. 'Where the hell do you keep the kleenex?' I hide the box, let them hunt in the bathroom. All the time with this ugly thing, waiting to be got rid of. 'Don't watch me.'

My father explained the moon now that it was captured inside a small TV. And she shuddered because even the moon had been touched by him. She dreaded his hands. God watched them both. Her God was an eye. Her God was shame.

Terrified on her wedding night, at least now she talks about it.

'Men and women were different then,' she says. 'No one knew anything. No one. Only whores.'

The passage into winter is the time when cracks between the seasons open, when something hideous might slip through in the dark. The sunlight squeezes out of the sky. Shadows hide things. There is the smell of danger with the first bonfire. We light candles to remember our dead. October turns into November: a time of ancestors, of spirits, of memory.

My turnip head grins. 'That's a good one,' she says. The yellow eyes are gouged out. We leave it in the shed at the end of the night. Unable to throw it out, for days after I creep down there to relight the stubs of candles. I do this every year until the head turns green. Wait until a fur mould covers the inside and the shell is soft and rotten. Even on the compost heap I watch my lantern sink, mouse haired, into grey and vanish.

She blames herself. She blames herself. 'If only ...' she'll say as this night draws on. She can't be left alone. We make the pilgrimage home each year. Strength in numbers she says and lights candles.

When did they stop speaking? It's hard to remember. It was gradual, crept up on them. One day they found themselves in silence.

We were out one evening. They stopped to talk to neighbours they disliked. I waited, scuffing the leather from my shoes. The women spoke, the men raised their eyebrows to each other. One of them must have touched a sore point. My parents had them like a prickly rash. She turned on him. 'You want to live in that shed of yours. You spend more time in it than anywhere.' And maybe she deserved what he did next, but the neighbours didn't. He began to speak as if she wasn't there; he said things like, 'Yes, Mr J., I married a woman who turned out to be the type that deliberately goes out of her way to place obstacles in front of me.' And there was Mrs J. nodding agreement the way you do when you haven't listened to a word someone's said, and catching herself on and blushing, staring at her husband, and he who was too embarrassed to fish her out. And my mother, staring at my father, as if she was having a conversation with him that no one else could hear. He just carried on. Then she walked away from him, picking up her feet carefully on the sharpened street.

Soft cracks opened up, silently, like whispers. They pulled her between them. Mute. Indoors the wallpaper was shredding, I heard it tear from the walls. When he spoke she tutted and turned away. When he entered a room she left it. Their movements became synchronised. As he reached across the table she shrank back. She wouldn't let him touch her.

'You don't understand!' she screams. 'In those days ... you didn't. Women weren't supposed to ... I hated it, every time, every time, I loathed it. How could he? How could he do that?'

She came running up the garden sobbing. She bolted the back door. 'You disgusting ... filthy ...' she choked. He had to let himself in through the front. He was silent.

Out of the window I had seen him cross the garden to the shed, he was hunched over, hands inside his coat. 'Where's that knife sharpener?' she'd asked. 'I'll bet your father has it. Run down and see.' But I wouldn't. Not this time. I'd seen him once, in the dank strange place he preferred to sit out in. There was this noise, rasping, and he was breathing like he was going into a fit, then I saw him arc backwards. I stepped away. He didn't see me. Some strange ritual, something to do with men. I told no one.

Years later I thought how sad it was and how pathetic – she surprised him looking for a knife sharpener.

My lovers always tell me not to stare. They get embarrassed. 'Some things are private,' one said, unrolling the pinkly glinting condom. And after. 'Where the hell do you keep the kleenex?'

But her face when she came into the house. The way she drew those bolts. She always told me women were punished for the fall. 'Torture,' she said. 'For Eve and her damned apple. We endure it. A punishment.'

I saw her running up the garden. Her sobs shook the ground. For days the looks she gave him. There was something shaming in the house. A new silence between them.

My lantern is finished. The shed door swings open and the lantern head rolls from my hand.

Again and again I watch it hit the stone floor. It smashes into pulp. It hits the stone floor. It bounces. The candle rolls out. The smell of the lid singeing, the sound of the skipping rope creaking.

I watch the lantern head hit the stone floor. It smashes into pulp. His tongue sticks out like a puppet's. It's dark and pitted. The colour of his skin is all wrong, blotched, purple. I can't find the switch and his eyes glint with the light coming from the kitchen. They pick up specks of hard shine like the industrial glass waste, and I think of the stuffed wolf in the museum, whose staring eyes are false and deadly.

The lantern head rolls from my hand. It hits the stone floor. It smashes into pulp.

I want to fly over the house, over this secret. Away to a different moon, one that he could never explain. I run and run through that tunnel of street and it touches me, the black softness strokes me. I see the pumpkin head smash to the ground. It has his face, the eyes are sightless, the soft flesh is scooped out, the place where memory is has been cut out and dumped. Behind those hollow eyes there is no feeling, no answer.

She can't be left alone on the anniversary. The train pulls fields behind it, streaked with grey. This is the danger time, when the fissures widen, when any of us might slip through the cracks between night and day, between the past and the present. We stay awake as long as we can, as if avoiding jet lag. When night comes we hope we'll sleep undisturbed till morning.

I remember the leather smell of seats in a police car. It was cold. There was a bright flashing light. Someone had wrapped me in a blanket. It was grey and scratched. They told me they found me in the park. She said her imagination had run riot. 'You never know what might have happened.'

For a long time no one said anything, only that he was

away. Whenever I asked, 'He's gone away.' Then later, 'He's gone to the angels.' There had been an accident.

Cause of death? We had a good Catholic doctor. They say the Irish are the happiest race in Europe. I checked the statistics. Seems we have less suicides.

My skipping rope vanished forever. My nightmares were of falling faces, of orange lantern heads. That was the last year we played those games.

And then I started to remember. But there's a different moon now, one that has been scorched, poisoned with science. Turns the roads into ash. A burning red moon, streaked like bloodshot.

They'll be waiting like they always do. The prodigal returns. I hate all this. Hate it. Pretend to be OK. Life good to me.

Looking back along the dark tunnel of street I can still smell the first bonfire of the season. Now that was something magical, that and the smell of chestnuts roasting, hot and hard to your hand then you peel them and they're yellow and waxy inside and there was always a good full yellow moon, like a chestnut waiting to be swallowed. There will be children out already, wailing and moaning, meeting other bands of ghost walkers just as we once laughed and frightened ourselves, shrieking with the delight of terror.

But she was always scared. And he had no time for those sort of games. Looking back, it's hard not to think that somehow they both always knew.

Moonwalk

ELLEN GALFORD

SUMMER IN the city, 1969, on the night of the day when men walk on the moon.

'Hey everybody on this bus,' says the wild-eyed hairy man, lurching towards the back (drunk, or, given the decade, maybe stoned or tripping). 'This moonshot. Today, on the TV news. All the channels, you can't get away from it. Men on the moon? Men on the MOON? MEN on the moon? Men ON the moon? Bull-plop! Horrrssse-puckey! Who they think they're kidding? It's all a fake. It's a movie. They're shooting in a studio downtown. By Canal Street. I delivered the coffee and donuts there this morning. Cat walks over, no, I swear to God, he bounces over to me in big space helmet and funny suit and boots and takes the bag, and it flies up towards the ceiling . . . and somebody screams CUT TO CAMERA THREE, YOU SCHMUCK, and they bang the door in my face and I don't even get no tip. It's a set-up. A big goddamned con! They're lyin' to us, lyin' in their fuckin' teeth . . . You hear me, America? . . . You hear me, world?? You hear me, people on this bus? . . . YOU HE-AR????'

Well, the driver hears. Without missing a chew of his gum,

19

he looks back down the bus through his rear-view mirror, pulls over, hits the brakes, swings the lever that opens the rear door. Then stomps down the aisle, hoists up the hairy man, and bellows in his face, 'We made it to the moon, buster. America got there first. You're the one telling lies!... No Commie bastard rides my bus. Take a hike, buddy!'

And throws him off.

They're on this bus, Suzanne and Larry and the rest, because they're going down to Chinatown for dinner. A favourite food-snob's place, deeply ethnic. Those curly ropes of orange-coloured pigs' innards, and the upside-down ducks with heads on, all hanging in the window, are guaranteed to put off your casual chop-suey-hunting tourist. The few round-eyes who penetrate feel possessive about it, and contemplate with loathing any fresh arrival of non-Chinese.

'God, this place is getting ruined...' mutters Larry. 'Ruined.'

'Yeah,' says Suzanne. 'Next thing you know they'll be printing the menu in English and handing out forks.'

It's a table for five. Suzanne has just married Larry ('It was a real gas, on this hillside upstate, everybody got stoned; we just did it for the presents, and to shut up our Moms'); they look alike, but his hair is even longer than hers. Larry works with Marcie, who's been going on and on about how she's dying to meet Suzanne, and how Larry would really lo-o-ve her husband Jeff, ('He's really into ethnic food, too').

Suzanne hates Jeff on sight. She can tell, just by the way he dresses, that he votes Republican and doesn't smoke dope; Marcie does, of course, she knows this from Larry's tales of Art Department outings to Central Park in the lunch break. But there's nothing really alternative about her either; Suzanne's slightly ashamed to be seen with them. Everything about them screams Suburban Young Marrieds.

The odd person out – and, Suzanne thinks, she really is odd – is this Irish chick. She's kind of a friend of a friend of a cousin of Marcie's, and she's passing through town, crashing at their place for a couple of nights on her way to see Amerika.

She must not come from the part of Ireland where they keep the Blarney Stone. She hardly says anything, just watches the rest of them, with a little wry corner-of-the-mouth smile. Suzanne gets the idea that if Larry and Jeff weren't around, she might have opened up more.

Things don't quite click. Marcie may think that Jeff is hot-stuff on ethnic restaurants, but compared to Suzanne and Larry, he doesn't have a clue. Even before they order, he starts on about how he's never been here himself, but it will have to go pretty far to beat Wing Wong Wei on Mott Street.

'Come on, man!' splutters Larry. 'Wing Wong Wei's complete crap.'

'So okay.' Jeff, leaning back in his chair, throws down the challenge. 'This is your place, guys; you picked it – you order. Show us what's good.'

Larry beckons to the waiter, who comes over and gives him a big hello, which does no harm at all for Larry's Chinatown street-cred. The waiter runs through the daily specials. Traditional moon festival foods feature largely. Not because of the Chinese calendar, but in honour of One Giant Step for Mankind. Duck braised with yams, very delicious, and big fat mooncakes with red-bean paste stuffing.

'We'll go,' says Larry, with a glance at Jeff, 'with that, plus some of the usual favourites.' And he lists everything he can think of that leaves the diner in no doubt as to its connections with death and disembowelment. Just daring Jeff to demur.

Suzanne checks the corner to see how all this goes down with the Irish girl; can't tell. She really wishes she knew what impression they were making.

When the food does come, it isn't as good as usual, and

21

Suzanne gets annoyed at the way Jeff smirks and says that he still rates Wing Wong Wei over this place, so she picks a fight with him about Vietnam. Tells him he's been brain-washed by the fascist-capitalist-death industry conspiracy. Jeff pounds his fist on the table and spills hot-and-sour soup over everything. How the hell was she supposed to know he used to be in the Marines?

The whole thing balloons up into a red-cooked, clear-simmered, chili-peppered, blazing hotpot of a screaming match, of the kind that are breaking up dinner tables all over the country around this time, with Larry yanking Suzanne by the sleeve and whispering, 'For chrissake, you want to get us thrown out of here and never allowed back?'

This is not what Suzanne wants. Suzanne wants to be somewhere very quiet, at a table for two in a moonlit pavement café overlooking the fountains of Rome or the bridges of Paris, getting the real low-down on the foreigner across the table.

Because Suzanne has been noticing certain women a lot lately. And wants them to notice her. This does not fit in with the hippie preacher on a hilltop, and the wedding presents and the thank-you letters and the mollified Moms.

'Listen, you guys,' says Marcie, desperate to make peace and turn chopsticks into ploughshares and rescue the evening, 'if we're gonna show Mary-Claire what this city's about, we gotta do the New York thing and go to Ferrara's.'

Because it would be a social disaster to end an evening this early, and because it is almost a Manhattan by-law that a Chinatown dinner shall be followed with a Little Italy dessert, everyone agrees. As if the Battle of the Big Muddy has never taken place over the mooncakes.

Walking up to Ferrara's, Larry grabs Suzanne's ass. 'How you doin', old lady?'

She reaches back and sweeps his hand away.

Slowing her pace, Suzanne tries to cut Mary-Claire out of the crowd, to lag behind the rest for a little one-to-one chat, but Marcie battens on. The guys are walking too fast for her. They, in turn, have swept the whole dinner fiasco under the carpet, and are talking moon-landing technicalities.

'Apollo, Apollo, Apollo. He's been on about goddamned Project Apollo since we got up this morning, hasn't he, Mary-Claire? I mean, it's fabulous and historic, but once you've said "Wow", what else is there to say?'

'I think it's rape, myself,' says Mary-Claire.

'Huh?'

'They should have left the old girl alone, and spent the money on famine relief.'

'That's exactly what I think,' announces Suzanne, who, until this very instant, hadn't.

'And,' adds Mary-Claire, 'the moon will never be the same again. They'll be leaving all sorts of rubbish up there.'

'What do you expect,' sneers Suzanne, 'typical men. Never think about cleaning up a mess.'

Marcie puts her hands up to her ears, giggles and goes 'Eeek! Jeff, hey Jeff, come back here and rescue me. These two are spouting that Women's Lib.'

'I've never seen or heard of any of the things on this menu,' says Mary-Claire.

'I'll order for you,' Suzanne offers. 'I know what's good here. I've tasted everything.'

'Tasted everything, have you?' Mary-Claire gives her a sidelong look. 'A woman of the world.'

When their orders come, Mary-Claire takes a long time to eat her cannoli, slowly teasing out nuggets of chocolate and candied fruit from the creamy filling. Mary-Claire watches Suzanne watching her and winks. 'Even nicer than Chinese mooncakes.'

Suzanne wishes she had a quick reply, all juicy with innuendo and secret signals.

'I really like your accent,' she says.

23

Mary-Claire blows at the peaked froth of her cappuccino.

Now Larry, on the other side, drops an arm around Suzanne's neck, and lassoes her back into the general conversation.

'Yeah, Suze and I saw it in the papers a couple of weeks ago, didn't we, babe? Fairies rioting.'

She is, momentarily, perplexed. She pictures a mêlée of tiny figures with gossamer wings and pink tutus, squeaking slogans and shaking star-topped wands, advancing upon ranks of big blue-coated policemen, while a fleet of furious Tinkerbells flash out of the heavens and strafe the fuzz from above.

'Oh, yeah, right. In the Village. When the pigs raided that gay bar ... Stonewood?'

'Stonewall,' Larry corrects her. 'Mrs Feather-brain.'

She is searching for a really neat put-down for Larry, when Jeff announces, 'I have to tell you, people, that's my least favourite thing about New York City. Too many fruits. You should see the pansy who lives in the apartment across the hall from us ... All he needs is a dress and a handbag. And upstairs, these, these two ... females ...'

'Creepy,' says Marcie. 'I hate it when we meet them in the elevator. I stand really close to Jeff, just in case.'

'Don't you kind of wonder,' Larry chuckles, 'which one – you know – plays the man ...?'

'Like, sick,' says Jeff. 'If scientists can get us to the moon, they ought to be able to find a cure for stuff like that.'

Mary-Claire slams her cup down, and stands up. She puts some money on the table. 'Listen, here's my share of the bill, and I'll just get a taxi back to your place, Marcie. I've the spare keys. My bus to Vermont leaves at the crack ... No need to break up everybody's evening on my account.'

Then off she goes.

'Well, that was sudden,' says Marcie.

'Weird chick,' shrugs Jeff.

But Suzanne's up, knocking over her chair with a clatter, and out the door straight after her. A taxi's right there, for once – luck of the Irish.

'Hey, wait!' bellows Suzanne, wrenching the yellow door back open before Mary-Claire can slam it. 'I'm coming too.'

'You are? I'm just going back up to Marcie's to pack my rucksack.'

'That's cool with me. Look, I'm sorry about those ... assholes.'

'Are you saying that husband of yours is an arsehole, too?'

'I don't know. Maybe. Yeah.'

The driver turns around. 'Hey listen, ladies, is this some kind of coffee-klatsch? Or are youse girls going somewhere? I don't mind – waiting time's extra on the meter. No skin off my nose. I'd just like to know. Because we're blocking traffic.'

'Tenth Avenue.'

With a screech of gears, they are off and racketing over the potholes.

'Hang on. Marcie's on East Seventy-eighth Street ...'

'I'm hijacking you. There's this great diner on the West Side. Open all night. We'll get some coffee. You never finished your cappuccino.'

'I told you, I have to leave at the crack of dawn.'

'And how long does it take to pack a rucksack? This is the city that never sleeps. You can catch a nap tomorrow, on the bus.'

In the floodlights of the concrete loading-bays, the chrome of the diner gleams. Two waitresses and some truck-drivers in baseball caps are leaning on the counter, talking about the men on the moon. A woman wearing a floral plastic shower-cap and a mink stole coos at a giant plush panda she has propped up on her table, as she tries to feed it pieces of blueberry muffin. Behind her sits a man with a prophet's robes, beard, and hypnotic gaze, swathed in an ornate assortment of veils, scarves, turbans and pendants, eating a bagel and cream-cheese.

'Jesus, Mary, and Joseph, what sort of a creature's that?' whispers Mary-Claire, as they slide into a booth.

'Hey,' says Suzanne, 'that's Moondog.'

'Who?'

'Crazy poet. He's usually over on Eighth Avenue, standing to attention and staring into space. This must be his coffee-break.'

One of the waitresses calls over to him. 'Hey, Moondog! What's your word on the astronauts?'

Moondog puts down his bagel, and softly howls.

'Stop staring,' hisses Suzanne. 'You want to look like a tourist?'

'I am a tourist,' says Mary-Claire.

'...It was probably a stupid thing to do,' says Suzanne, three cups of coffee later. 'It's not like we want to go off and be mommy and daddy in the suburbs like Marcie. I think I'm sort of against it, on political grounds. But there were reasons. I'd been going through some very heavy head-trips. And then my mother got sick ... and then ... well, some things happened, and I almost got raped coming home from the laundromat one night, and good old Larry really helped me through that – I've known him since freshman year. It felt safe.'

'You don't have to justify yourself to me.'

'I don't know why. But I want to.'

Mary-Claire concentrates on stirring sugar into her cup. 'You're a grown-up, you make your own decisions...'

'I used to think twenty-two was grown-up, until I got here.'

'I'm twenty-five, and I don't expect to grow up till I'm ninety.'

'You seem pretty together to me.'

'Just a façade. Wait till you get to know me better.'

26

'And how am I supposed to do that?' Suzanne glances at the clock above the chrome coffee-machine. 'You're leaving in six hours.'

'Well, as you said yourself, this is the city that never sleeps.'

'Down in the Village,' says Suzanne, 'there are these late-night bars where ... I've never been to one myself, but I'm sure if we go down to Christopher Street, we can ask around and ...'

'No thanks. Sorry to disappoint you, if that's what you had in mind. I'm not really interested in the bars.'

'But I thought ...'

'You thought it was a requirement for membership, did you?'

'Well ...' Suzanne dips her head so her long hair hides the blush, then searches out strands with split ends.

'Well, allow me to complete your education ...'

Suzanne, head up, surprises herself with the look she flashes her. 'I wish you would.'

They don't hurry, making their way eastwards and uptown.

It is after five a.m. when they reach the white-brick apartment house where Marcie and Jeff live.

'Christ,' sneers Suzanne, after they have identified themselves to a sleepy doorman, walked through a lobby filled with tubs of ailing plants, and are riding upwards in a mirrored box. 'It's even more petty-bourgeois pretentious than I expected ... Sorry to say this, but your friend Marcie ...'

'Stop apologising. I hardly know the woman. It's the usual distant connections ... If you're ever in New York, look up my cousin's old flatmate sort-of-thing ...'

'I'm hip. We had this really amazing experimental dance-troupe from Finland sleeping on our floor a couple of months ago ... It was all because someone Larry used to ...'

When the elevator door slides open, Larry himself is

standing in the corridor, barring the way to Jeff and Marcie's door.

'Where the fuck have you been?'

Jeff sticks his head out. 'Hey, keep it down! You'll wake the neighbours!'

Inside the apartment, Jeff and Marcie pretend to be very casual, fussing over the choice of album.

'Jefferson Airplane? Simon & Garfunkel?'

'I think I'd better get organised,' mutters Mary-Claire, and disappears.

'What kind of stunt was that? We've been waiting here for hours, going frantic. Why didn't you call me?'

'Well if you've been hanging around up here, instead of going home, how do you know I didn't?'

'Because I know.'

'And how could I have called here, because I don't know the number, because I never even met these people until tonight? They're your goddamn friends!'

Someone in the next-door apartment starts banging on the wall.

'If you ever listened to a word I said,' Larry roars, 'you'd have known Marcie's last name, and you'd have known she lived on East Seventy-eighth Street, and you could have asked Information to give you the number. Or you could have asked that dykey pal of yours...'

'She's...'

'Well, she is, as it happens,' interrupts Mary-Claire, reappearing with her rucksack. 'Dykey as they come. And I haven't the faintest idea, or interest, in what you'll all make of that. I'll be off to the bus terminal now, Marcie. Thanks very much for the last couple of nights.'

'Gosh, Mary-Claire, I never thought ... you know you don't look like...'

Jeff puts a protective hand on Marcie's shoulder. 'Shut up, Marcie. The woman wants to get her bus.'

'Okay, let's go,' says Suzanne.

'And where do you think you're off to?' Larry grabs her arm. She shakes loose.

'Port Authority's full of creeps and weirdos even in the daytime. I'm not letting Mary-Claire hang around there by herself at this hour. Cool it. I'll be home for breakfast. I'll bring hot croissants from the place on Second Avenue...'

They are silent in the taxi, jaws clenched with terror as the driver, eyes like whirling pinwheels, scrapes the paint off half a dozen other cars and shreds his brakes on the headlong flight downtown.

'Land of the living dead,' says Suzanne, inside the bus terminal, as someone staggers towards them, flapping his torn raincoat like wings and screaming, 'God will punish you human bastards for defying his laws and stepping on the moon. The moon will explode and all of earth will be drowned in the fiery molten tears of Beelzebub and beware those who fornicate and...'

'Thanks for coming with me,' says Mary-Claire, sidestepping a man who reaches out a beckoning arm, waggles his tongue between his lips and chants, 'Here chickie, chickie, chickie. P-o-o-o-ntang!'

'Welcome to Hell,' says Suzanne.

'I'd heard this place was a little unsavoury, but...'

'But you're a big strong girl, and you could have taken care of yourself... I know, I know...'

'That's not what I was going to say at all. I'm glad you came.'

'Once we find the right ticket-window,' says Suzanne, 'maybe we'll go hang out in the ladies' until bus-time. There's sort of a waiting-room in there. It is, just marginally, less paranoid than anywhere else.'

In the ladies' lounge, they watch two young women changing.

Almost in sync, the pair, standing at a wide mirror, brush back their long, loose hair into tight French twists, slip off long, loose gypsy gowns and zip on neat navy-blue skirts, take the Indian toe-rings and Egyptian scarabs off their fingers, kick off their sandals and wriggle into panty-hose, fish in their bags for high-heeled pumps, tie scarves stamped with a company logo in pussy-cat bows at their necks, rub off kohl eye-liner and re-paint their lids in a chaste sky-blue, imprint their lips with a pale pink kiss-colour and blot them dry. Then, after checking the mirror to assess the room's other occupants – most of them huddled on the benches and snoring – one dips into a shoulder bag and brings out a joint.

'What a night,' she says. 'I'm still flashing.'

Her friend lights the joint, yawning. 'We all out of speed? God knows how I'll make it to lunch hour.'

They heel-clack to the door, one nearly tripping over Mary-Claire's rucksack. 'Goddammit.'

'Bye-bye and God bless you, darlings.' An old woman, surrounded by creased and overflowing bags, makes a sign of benediction at the slamming door. Then she turns her attention to Suzanne and Mary-Claire. 'I watch everybody come and go,' she tells them. 'Saint John the Baptist pays me thirty-five dollars a week to watch the ladies'. Those two, you two, any two, anyone. Hoors and virgins and boys with false titties thinking nobody can tell. My daughter put me here and told me not to move. Nineteen-fifty-five, you'd think she'd be back from making that phone call to Cincinnati by now. But I know what's happening. Nothing passes me by.' She rises, gathers up her bundles. 'Saint John the Baptist says I got to go now. Time to watch the orange juice bubble up in the machine at Walgreen's. That's how I get my instructions. Now you two behave yourselves. Bye-bye.'

'Well,' whispers Mary-Claire, after a while, 'there's a nice little *memento mori* for you.'

'Shit,' says Suzanne, after an even longer while. 'Shit.

Nothing like a good old grisly fairy-tale to scare someone off from ever leaving home.'

They are sitting very close together, side-by-side, as if already jammed on the seat of a bus going somewhere. Suzanne tries to keep everything bottled up, but she can tell that Mary-Claire feels her shaking.

'Are you all right?'

Suzanne doesn't let herself answer for a minute. Then says, 'Hey, listen. You remember, down in Little Italy, walking up to Ferrara's . . .'

'That would be a few lifetimes ago by now, wouldn't it?'

'You know how you said that the moon had been – like, raped, by the men on her.'

'Ye-e-s . . .'

'Well, do you think she'll ever be the same again?'

'How could she?'

'Does that mean you think it's ruined her, forever?'

Mary-Claire stares off into space for a minute. Then looks at Suzanne.

'And why should the moon care what I think at all?'

Suzanne doesn't answer.

'Well, this is what I think. The moon's a big place. They only touched a few bits. Hardly saw anything of her, and didn't understand what they did see. And they never made it to the dark side, did they? That's hers, for herself. And that's the side that interests me.'

She twines her fingers with Suzanne's.

'Damn,' says Suzanne.

'Damn what?'

'This is the wrong place to be just now.'

'I could think of a more romantic setting, but never mind.'

'I've been thinking, for a long time, about . . . well, you know . . . Oh, god, I can't say this . . . I, you know . . .'

'You credit me with telepathic gifts, do you? I hope I'm right. Because I know that, if someone were wanting to kiss, be

31

kissed by, a woman for the first time in her life, not a quick little kiss, but a serious kiss, with as much attention paid to it as it justly deserves, then she certainly would not want it to happen in the Port Authority Terminal ladies' room.'

'No, I guess not.'

'So why don't you just buy yourself a bus ticket, and get on that Greyhound with me, and come along up to Vermont?'

'Do you have even the faintest idea of how much I want to?'

'Well, perhaps just the faintest idea.' Mary-Claire looks at her watch. 'And I wouldn't put any pressure on you, but it's got to happen now, if it's going to happen ... Because, much as I delight in your company, the next bus doesn't go until four in the afternoon.'

They walk back along the concourse to the escalators. The lost souls of the night have been joined by the first trickle of morning commuters.

'Well, there's the Greyhound ticket window.'

Suzanne stands still for a minute. 'I want to . . .'

'Good.'

'I'm really tempted . . .'

'I'm flattered.'

'But, if I go with you this minute, things are going to be – very messy.'

'They're going to be very messy whenever you decide to go.'

'You didn't say if.'

'I know.'

At the platform, Suzanne says, 'Hang on. This commune ... where your friends live ... Does it have anything so decadent and capitalistic as a phone?'

Mary-Claire pulls a piece of printed paper from her pocket. 'Got a pen?' She writes the number on the margin. 'If I'm not there, because I'm travelling, they'll know where I am.'

32

Suzanne puts her hand on Mary-Claire's arm. 'Hey listen, when a Greyhound bus leaves ... it's usually going someplace faraway. So it's all right for people seeing off people to give them a goodbye kiss. Even in the land of God and Mom and Napalm and Apple Pie, they don't usually arrest you for it.'

'All right, then.'

It takes a while for it to be over. But Suzanne doesn't think it's half long enough.

'Well ...' she catches her breath, and looks around, at a few suitcase-carrying stragglers from the straight world, staring. 'I think they might just make an exception, and arrest us for that one.'

'I'd better get aboard then, before they start stoning the bus.'

'Was it all right, though?'

'Daft question.'

'I mean, did I do it right?'

'It was perfect. Sweet as honey ... No, sweeter even than mooncakes.'

The bus driver hits his horn, and makes them both jump, to hurry her up.

In the taxi, going cross-town, Suzanne pulls out the paper to look at the phone number. She sees that Mary-Claire has written it on the schedule for the Vermont bus.

'Hey, sister,' chirps the cab-driver, one of the talkative kind, 'Did you see those Apollo guys on TV? ... Amazing, yeah?'

'Well,' says Suzanne, 'not many people know this, but I'll let you in on a little secret. They never went to the moon. It's all a big CIA-type conspiracy, man. Just like the assassination of JFK. The whole thing was a con, to keep us distracted while they're up to some kind of sinister political business somewhere down here ... They did it all with trick photography. Special effects. Movie cameras, in a film studio near

Chinatown... I have this on very good authority. You think about it, mister, and ask yourself, can you actually prove, beyond a shadow of a doubt, that what you saw on the TV was real?'

The cabbie knows better than to argue with a lunatic. In New York, even a female crazy can pull a gun.

'Okay, okay, okay, doll. All right already. You win. No men on the moon.'

Manskin, Womanskin

LISA TUTTLE

HE SAID, 'I think we'd be more comfortable in the bedroom, don't you?' and I said, 'Where's the loo?'

It was our first time alone together in his house and we both knew what we were there for. We'd met at a friend's party and had gone out together seven times in three weeks. Although we were still on our best behaviour, and I was aware that I still knew very little about him, the urge to get closer was strong, very strong. A lot is made of the loss of virginity as a great moment of decision, as a trauma, even, but the loss of mine had been easy and inevitable, and my first boyfriend and I had been together for nearly eight years. Making up my mind to go to bed with my second boyfriend had been much more difficult, and now I felt that I had taken too long and been over-cautious. I'd been so determined not to make a mistake, to be certain that this relationship would last – and in the end we'd broken up after less than two years. This time, although I still wanted it to be the last first time, this man my final one-and-only, I'd decided to take a chance and be a little braver about the unknown.

After three weeks of increasing warmth and interest the time was right. I was nervous, but willing. I'd meant to conquer my nervousness by staying close to him, so close that clothed kisses on the sofa would progress without any major break to the naked intimacies in his bed. But when you've gotta go, you've gotta go. So off I went and didn't realise until the door was closed with me inside the little room that the light-switch was on the wall outside. But I didn't need light for what I had to do, and if I had, the moonlight sifting dreamily through frosted glass would have been enough.

I wondered, as I sat on the pot, if Fred was as nervous as I was. It seemed unlikely. He was thirty-nine, ten years older than me, and he'd never been married. Although he hadn't itemised his girlfriends for me, I gathered there had been quite a few. He didn't seem to have much luck with sustaining relationships, a fact about which he seemed rueful and a bit bewildered. It was obvious to me that he just hadn't met the right woman. Was I the right woman? I thought of the sense of intimacy and understanding between us already, despite the fact that we'd known each other only three weeks. Was it a false understanding? Sexual attraction was like moonlight, casting a glamour on things that would look terribly ordinary in daylight, like that garment, whatever it was, hanging from a hook on the back of the bathroom door. The moonlight made it look like a cast-off human skin, if humans could cast off their skins.

I remembered a movie I wished I'd never seen, about a psycho who murdered women for their skins, and I jumped up. I felt a little sick. Yet there was nothing grisly or horrible about the thing. When I touched it, it was so cool and fine between my fingertips that it might have been spun from the moonlight itself.

It came down from the hook into my hands as if I wanted it, and the sensation of all that impossibly light mass tumbling into my arms made me dizzy with desire. I just had to put it on.

It was the weirdest sort of garment I'd ever encountered, a full body suit with hands and feet and head. It seemed all of a piece, yet as soon as I looked for an opening it was open in my hands, inviting me out of my clumsy, constricting clothes and inside it. There was no zip or other form of fastening, yet when I pressed the edges of the skin together they bonded fast. It seemed that a light veil had fallen over my face, I could feel something lighter than the finest silk against my skin, yet there was no obstruction. I could breath as freely as ever, open and shut my eyes, even open my mouth and put out my tongue. I thought my vision was slightly affected, as if veiled, yet that may have been the moonlight.

I ran my hands over my naked/not naked body, finding it both familiar and strange. I had changed, the skin had changed me, but I was still myself. For the first time in my life I knew, absolutely, that I was beautiful, and, for the first time since childhood, felt completely at home in my body. No longer nervous, I went out to meet my lover.

He was waiting for me in the bedroom, in the moonlight which streamed through net curtains, as naked as I was. His unexpected handsomeness took my breath away. His body was more impressive than his clothes revealed, and the shadows chiseled what I'd first thought were the fairly ordinary – though very nice – features of his round face into more pleasing, classical proportions. I should have felt utterly intimidated by the sight of this stranger, but instead I was engulfed by a wave of lust that carried all my qualms and hesitancies out to sea, and washed me onto the bed, into his arms.

The first time I tried to make bread it was awful. I felt clumsy and irritable, did everything wrong, and in the end I threw the batch out. After that, it was fine. In fact, baking bread is one of my favourite things to do. But my first experience with it sums up my attitude towards first times in bed with someone new:

it'll be awful, but worth it in the long run. Since there's no way of avoiding the first time, you might as well just be as relaxed as you can about it, get through it, perform the mental equivalent of throwing it out uneaten, and take your reward from the pleasures to come.

Things I'd heard from my friends made me believe it was true for everyone – certainly for all women – but *that* first time, in the skin, was totally different. Our bodies seemed to recognise each other, our bodies *adored* each other, and it was impossible to put a hand or a foot or anything else wrong. All, all was mutual delight.

It was the skin, of course, but while I was in it, I thought it was me. A me wonderfully, gloriously changed, but still me.

I fell asleep in the skin. In the morning, I'd forgotten I had it on, but in the bathroom, just as I was about to step into the shower, the skin suddenly fell away from me, running down my body and dropping smooth as water to puddle at my feet.

I picked it up and examined it in the dull and murky daylight. It was a silvery no-colour, like a snake's shed skin, but without brittleness. Fine, supple and strong, it had no weight, almost no mass. I crushed it into the palm of my hand, closed my fingers on it until it was invisible and felt like nothing at all. I could carry it in my purse or pocket, keep it with me always, I thought – then I hung it back on the door where I'd found it.

In the kitchen, amid the smells of coffee and charred toast, Fred looked ordinary again, ordinary and a little shy, and I knew that must be how I looked, too. He didn't seem to mind, though. He seemed to like looking at me, and he didn't avoid my eye, rather he caught it, and smiled.

An accidental bump led to a fervent clutch and a kiss and very soon, clutching and groping at each other, we made our way back down the hall to the bedroom. He seemed different in daylight, the whole thing was different, clumsier and sweatier, no less urgent yet somehow scarier, a new first time. And then he paused and drew back a little. 'Shall we ... uh, do you want to ... ?'

'Of course.' I rolled away from him just enough to reach the box of condoms on the table, but when I looked back I could see that wasn't what he meant. 'No?'

'Oh, yes, that too, but I meant – like last night. In the skins.'

It shocked me to hear him say it. How could I have thought it was my secret when it was his house I'd found it in? Yet, since it had fallen off the memory of the womanskin had moved into the part of my mind where dreams and sexual fantasies lived, and to have Fred refer to it gave me the creepiest feeling, as if he'd somehow got inside my head.

He misinterpreted the look on my face. 'Of course we don't have to, if you didn't like it. I thought it was rather special, that's all ...'

'Yes, yes, I did too.' Belatedly I twigged. '*You* were wearing one, too!'

'Yes, of course.'

'Fred, what are they?' I rolled onto my side, propping myself up on an elbow, and he mirrored me.

'I don't know. A manskin and a womanskin, just what they seem to be. No, honestly, I don't know any more than you do.'

'You must. Where did they come from?'

'I don't know. I found them in the garden.'

'In your garden?' I looked at the bedroom window, still curtained in net, at the greenish blur beyond. I hadn't seen his garden yet, but I was familiar enough with the pocket-handkerchief gardens of this neighbourhood of London to imagine the narrow, fenced-in rectangle of grass bounded on at least two sides by flower-beds or shrubberies, all most unmagical. 'You found them in your garden? How? When? Tell me, Fred!'

'Well, did you think I'd bought them in a shop?' He grinned at me. 'The garden's nothing special; I'll show you later. There's a little shed down at the bottom, and a compost heap; the skins were lying on the grass in between. It was about a month ago – well, it must have been exactly a month ago because the moon was full, like it was last night. It was about a week before we met – you see, I haven't had them very long. I was feeling a little lonely and a little restless and I wasn't quite ready to go to bed, although it was late enough. It wasn't raining and I could see the moon shining away when I went to draw the curtains, so I thought I'd go out into the garden for a breath of air. That was when I saw something shining like moonlight on the grass. It looked like – you know, quicksilver? That's what I thought of, quicksilver flowing in the shape of a person. Like a shadow on the grass, but light instead of dark, almost like a concentrated essence of light, shining up from the dark grass. I went over to it and bent down to touch it, and it was as I was lifting it up that it fell apart into two, and I realised I was holding – well, you know.'

'So you just kept them?'

'What would you have done?'

'Did you try them on?'

'Just the manskin,' he said swiftly, so swiftly that the qualification made me wonder. 'Once I had it on I knew that it was no good by itself, that they were meant to be a couple, were for a couple.'

'So a few days later you asked me out.'

'I would have asked you out anyway. It might have taken me a little longer, that's all. The skin gave me an extra – it gave me courage.'

'And then yesterday you left the womanskin hanging on the back of the bathroom door hoping – what? That I'd just see it and happen to try it on?'

He nodded.

'What if I hadn't?'

'But you did.' He smiled his sweet, shy smile. 'Shall we put them on again?'

I wasn't feeling the slightest bit sexy, the mood had gone to something else entirely, and I wanted to go on exploring it, exploring him by talking, but I was so moved by his strange story, and by him, that I did what he said, got up and went to the bathroom and slipped into the womanskin. I knew as soon as I returned that he was wearing his – there was nothing to see, but I sensed it, like an aura. As soon as the two skins came into contact they began making love. Of course it was *we* who did all those things, our two bodies fitting together as if we'd been lovers for years, and of course we experienced the arousal, the growing excitement, the climax, and yet all the while there was some small part of me which remained remote, aware that Fred and I were two strangers, separated by the skins, and that all the passion they generated had nothing really to do with us.

At first, in the beginning days and weeks of our deepening relationship, I didn't like to say anything about it. Sex in the skins was so reliably wonderful that it seemed sheer perversity to ask to try it without them. And besides, I thought naked sex was bound to happen naturally before long – we'd just get carried away and do it without thinking of the skins.

But it didn't. If we were caught in the throes of passion on the couch in the middle of watching the late-night movie, we had to pause for contraception, and given a pause, the skins would insert themselves. I could have protested, of course, made a joking or a serious request to leave them out of it. But I guess I wanted it to come from Fred. I was afraid of finding out that the skins meant more to him than I did.

Every night Fred would slip into his skin at bedtime, the way that I might have inserted my diaphragm, just in case. But there was no 'just in case' about it, because once he'd put the manskin on, I seemed to feel a yearning from the womanskin which would have been cruel to ignore. I couldn't just be myself when Fred had on the manskin; I had to be her.

They were no good on their own, the skins. It was as Fred had told me, they were a couple, made for a couple. One morning I had the notion of wearing the womanskin out into the world, of going to work in it and seeing how other people would react. But I couldn't do it. The skin which clasped me so close whenever I was alone with Fred simply refused to stay on; it would not be worn under clothes or without sexual intent.

I don't mean to imply that the skins dominated our lives. The skins were only for sex, and when we weren't wearing them, or about to, even the memory of them seemed to slip away, at least from me. There's always more to life than sex, even in the most passionate relationship. Fred and I began to spend all our spare time together. Although I still, cautiously, continued to pay rent on my single room, and left my out-of-season clothes hanging in the wardrobe there, I was effectively living with him. I met his friends and he met mine, we cooked for each other and went shopping together, joked and argued and shared a life. It should have been perfect – the sex could not have been better – yet I felt there was something missing. I wanted a greater closeness. Fred didn't know what I meant. How could we be closer? We did everything together and the sex, every night, was great. I thought maybe we should talk more about ourselves. Fred didn't, but he did his best to oblige, answering my questions about his past, or what he felt about something, even when I could tell he found them annoying or unimportant or intrusive.

I couldn't explain what was wrong, what was missing, but something was. After a while I became obsessed with the notion that the skins were coming between us, and that the intimacy I craved would be ours only if we made love without them.

Of course, I should have said something about how I was feeling, but our love was still too new: I didn't want him to think I was dissatisfied, or to make him unhappy. So, in time-honoured female fashion, I resorted to trickery.

We were on our way to the cinema, a route which took us right past the house where I rented a room, when I suddenly expressed a need for a particular sweater I'd left there. Obligingly he went along with me, and as soon as we were together behind the closed door of my room I faked an overwhelming passion to get us onto my single bed. But even before all our clothes were off he'd revealed that, alongside the emergency condom I already knew he carried in his wallet, he also carried both the skins.

'They fold down to nothing at all, you must have noticed,' he said. 'I don't always carry them with me, but this morning I just thought I'd see if they'd fit ... lucky chance, huh?'

I burst into tears and confessed. He was astonished. Why hadn't I said?

Now, too late, I tried to make light of my desire. I hadn't asked because I hadn't wanted to make it seem important. It wasn't important. Our relationship, most particularly the sexual side of it, was wonderful. Only, now and then I wondered if we might not be even closer if we made love without the skins. Hadn't he ever wondered about that, about how it would feel?

He said he had not. He said he couldn't imagine being any closer to anyone than he already was to me. He said that sex with me, in the skins, was the best he'd ever known and, that being so, why should he want anything different? But now that he knew what I wanted ...

Now that he knew what I wanted, we had to do it there and then, the skins folded back into his wallet. Was it their presence, like uninvited ghosts, which made what followed so unsatisfactory? Or was it my guilt at having tried to deceive him? How could I complain we weren't close enough when I kept my own feelings hidden? It was a pretty wretched coupling, all told. I'd seldom felt less like having sex, and it was easy to imagine the pressures on Fred struggling to satisfy me unaided. No wonder that we ended up farther apart, more

43

alone than ever. No wonder it was such a relief to put the skins on again later that night and feel ourselves drawn back together. In my imagination the skins had been coming between us, blocking a more perfect understanding, but now I could see it was the skins which saved us from our differences. Without the skins we were only ordinary. With them we were special.

We soon took great sex for granted, as our right. We were spoiled by the skins which made sex instant and easy and completely detached from the rest of life. It still made me uneasy because it was so unnatural. We were in the unlikely situation of being in a sexual relationship in which the sexual part was completely unaffected by the relationship.

The sex was magic, but the sex belonged to the skins. It didn't matter if we'd just been arguing about whose turn it was to clean the bathroom; or whether someone who voted Conservative could be, in any sense of the word, a *good* person; it didn't matter if he was tired or I had a hangover – whatever our moods, whatever our differences, if we put on the skins we were instantly ready for love. The skins took us into another world, their world, where only one thing mattered. Tiredness, anger, irritation, menstrual cramps either vanished or stopped mattering for a little while. Yet it was the same if I was feeling particularly loving towards Fred for some reason, or if I was already aroused by some fantasy I'd been having – none of it mattered, nothing made any difference, positive or negative, in the realm of the skins. Fred and I were involved in a sexual relationship, but it was not our own.

Our relationship did not influence the sex, but the sex definitely influenced our relationship. It's hard to share several hours of physical bliss with someone and not feel, at the very least, *warm* towards them the next day. Kitchen and bathroom foibles, odd and even disgusting personal habits are easily forgiven in the afterglow, differences forgotten because unimportant. I don't know what sort of lovers we would have been without the skins; neither of us was eager to find out, unwilling to spoil what we did have. And yet there were times when I was with Fred when I felt lonelier than I'd ever felt on my own. I put it down to hormones.

I still don't know why I put on the manskin one night. Opportunity, I suppose, and curiosity. I had never examined it, I don't think I'd ever even touched it except when Fred was wearing it. We'd just been getting ready for bed when the telephone rang and he went out of the room to answer it, leaving his skin lying on the bed.

Wondering how different it was to mine, I picked it up, and, because I was naked already, put it on.

I didn't expect it to fit. My skin fit me, as his fit him, as if they'd been specially tailored to our proportions, and Fred was nearly six inches taller than I was, with broader shoulders and longer arms. Yet the manskin settled onto my nakedness like my own skin. Looking down at myself, I thought there'd been some mix-up: his skin couldn't possibly fit me so tightly and comfortably. This must be a woman's skin.

But I knew it wasn't mine. Fred had been wearing this skin; it was unmistakably his. Something of his essence still clung to it the way that a smell, perfume or body odour, will cling to much-worn, unwashed clothes. This wasn't a smell, though; it was emotion, it was personality, it was cast of mind, a sort of echo of Fred himself, which I recognised as surely as I recognised his voice on an answering machine, his arms around me in a dark room.

It was almost like being Fred, knowing what he knew, feeling what he felt. It was intimacy beyond anything I'd ever experienced, a way of knowing what I'd only struggled to imagine, before, and the knowledge overwhelmed me with love.

Fred came back into the room and I tossed him my skin. 'Put it on,' I said. 'Quickly!'

I don't think he understood what I had done until he had

put it on. I saw the astonishment on his face, the melting into love, in the minute or so before we came together to make love.

It was the best ever. In the past I'd sometimes felt more like a passenger than a participant, aware that it could be someone else, anyone else, inside without making any difference to what was happening between manskin and womanskin. Great sex, yet somehow anonymous.

This could not have been less anonymous. I was engulfed by Fred himself, by the sensual, sensory memories of the man. I was in *his* skin, and yet I was myself, making love to him, the man I felt with every part of me, in *my* skin. Words can't explain or do it justice. I'm not even sure I can really remember it now, not the way it really was, but one thing is certain: it was the high-point of our love-affair.

The problem with heights is that once you've reached the highest there is nowhere to go but down. The next few nights afterwards we made love the old way: Fred in the manskin, I in the womanskin, until I began to grow restless and want something more.

When I suggested we swop skins, Fred was adamantly opposed. I didn't quite believe his opposition – it had been so wonderful, how could he not want it again? I teased and pressed and pestered for a reason.

'It's not right, that's why. It's not natural.'

'Oh, and the skins are?'

'Of course they are!' He glared at me. 'I can understand curiosity, once, but you should be satisfied now. Aren't you satisfied with being a woman?'

'But it's not about being a woman! I'm still a woman, with the skin or without it – whichever skin I wear. It doesn't make any difference.'

'If it doesn't make any difference, why do you want to wear the manskin?'

'It's not about being a man or a woman, it's about being you. Well, *feeling* you, knowing you better than— Knowing you from the inside. That's what it's like; that's why I liked it. Not because it was a *man*skin – really, I couldn't tell any difference between them – but because it was yours. Didn't you like being in my skin?'

'It's not your skin, it's just something I let you wear. And no, I didn't like it particularly. I don't like feeling like a woman. I'm a man.'

I was suddenly frightened, aware that I was on dangerous ground. All at once the skins were his and I was – who was I, what was I, to him?

'Of course you're a man. It's because you *are* a man, and I'm not, and it's because I love you, that I want to know you in every way there is. I want to get closer to you, I don't want to take anything away from you—'

'Then you shouldn't try. Loving me isn't wanting to *be* me; it isn't wanting to turn me into a woman. If you really loved me you'd want to be even *more* of a woman, to make me feel more of a man. That's what the skins are all about.'

'I'm sorry.' It was hard for me to accept the truth, that what had been for me a high point of intimacy and understanding had been no such thing for him. Instead of feeling closer to me in my skin he had simply felt, unhappily, like a woman. Any woman, I guess, with me as any man. I gave up trying to explain it to him. If he didn't want to be inside my skin I wasn't going to try to force him.

After that we made love less often. His aversion to wearing the womanskin created an ambivalence in me, an insecurity. Was the woman he had encountered traces of in the skin so unloveable? Who did he imagine that I was? We made love a few times without the skins in pursuit of our old closeness but it was never satisfactory. We tried very hard for a time and then we gave up trying.

We were drifting apart. The term implies a gradualness, and it was certainly not abrupt, yet it happened very quickly once it began. Both of us became busy with things that kept us out of the house and out of each other's way. I went back to my room more often, and even spent the night there, especially if I was going out with friends after work or if he said he would be out late.

Yet it wasn't easy, giving up on Fred. I'd always liked being part of a couple, and I'd never entered a relationship without intending it to last forever. And I missed him. Memories of the early days of our romance haunted me, memories of intimacy, wordless feelings I would never have again.

Neither of us said anything about what was happening, reluctant to bring it to a formal, final close. We spent two or three nights a week together, and although I had been gradually, unobtrusively shifting my things back to my own room, I still had my own key to his house.

One evening which we had planned to spend together I happened to get there first. I took my bottle of wine into the kitchen, and then went down the hall to the bathroom.

The skins, both of them, were hanging from the hooks on the back of the door. It gave me quite a start to see them, for Fred had long been in the habit of folding his carefully away after use. When it wasn't in his wallet he kept it in a small, round, leather stud-box on the bedroom dresser. I had tended to leave the womanskin hung on the back of the door where I'd first found it, but after feeling his disapproval of 'picking up after me' a few times, I'd found a Chinese red silk purse and used that faithfully. I was sure that I'd folded it away after the last time; certainly the skins had not been hanging in the bathroom when I left on Sunday night.

Then I noticed that they were moving. It was only the faintest of gentle waving motions, as if they stirred in a breeze, but there was no breeze in the closed room, and if there had been, it would have impelled the skins to move both in the same direction not, as I could plainly see, in gentle flutterings towards each other.

What I saw, and I knew it, was pure yearning. They longed

for each other all the time, but only by human intervention could they come together. We could live without them, but they needed us.

I lifted them down from their hooks, took them into the bedroom, and lay them flat on the bed, one on top of the other. I watched for a little while but there was no visible movement – maybe, for them, no movement was necessary now they were so close. Then, feeling embarrassed by my own curiosity, I left the room, turning out the light when I went.

Fred and I had dinner in – a take-away from the local Indian – and then watched a production of *Don Giovanni* on television. Opera is not really my sort of thing, and he had offered to tape it and watch it by himself later, but I was getting the prickly sensation that Fred had decided it was time at last for our serious talk, and I was grateful for anything that would postpone it. Our relationship was nearly over, but I was determined it should last long enough for us to make love once more.

When we went into the bedroom together he looked startled at the sight of the skins on the bed.

'Oh, maybe not,' he said. 'Maybe it wouldn't be such a good idea tonight – I've been meaning to talk to you—'

'Later. Don't say anything now. We'll put on the skins – we could be any man, any woman – we can talk tomorrow.'

Hastily I stripped off my clothes, knowing that once I was in the skin he wouldn't argue with me, he would feel the yearning, too, and the compulsion to satisfy it.

Then I was in the skin and – it wasn't mine anymore. All at once I was suffocatingly close to, intimate with, a complete stranger. It was like waking up in the middle of a rape, and the worst part about it was the hot, heavy desire all around – I felt it as if it was mine, and it was directed at Fred – but I knew it belonged to somebody else. I wanted to scream but I couldn't. Somehow I managed to peel the thing off me, and then I stood naked, trembling, staring outraged at my lover.

'You've had someone else here – you've been making love with someone else!'

'I was going to tell you – I tried—'

'You were going to tell me! And that makes it all right?'

'Oh – please. Don't go all – as if I'd broken your heart. You know perfectly well that things were already all but finished between us.' His calm, weary, rational tone made me aware that I was playing a role lifted from soap opera, but I couldn't seem to stop.

'All but, yes. All but. But not completely finished. It would have been nice if you could at least have waited, instead of ending it like this, humiliating me, and – and why did you have to bring her here? Why did you have to use the skins?'

He stopped looking defensive.

'You know why,' he said quietly. 'You know perfectly well why. The same reason you dragged me in here and tore off all your clothes ten minutes ago. Nothing to do with love for me. Nothing much to do with you, either.'

Anger and hurt rushed out of me like air from a pricked balloon, leaving me limp. I began to put my clothes back on. 'I wasn't the first, was I?'

He sighed and shook his head. 'But it felt like the first time with you, it really did. That's all I meant. I didn't want you thinking it was routine, or old hat, or— Because it really was special with you, like the very first time.'

'Did you really find them in your garden?'

'Different garden. Down in Suffolk. Years ago – the night I lost my virginity. Some fifty-odd women ago.'

I was all dressed now. I looked at my watch, saw that the underground would still be running. I could go home. 'Well – good luck. I hope you're happy. Maybe she'll be the one.'

He smiled a little, mocking my conventional expectations. 'That's not what it's about. I don't need *one*.'

Can't Help It

SARAH SCHULMAN

        I WAS born Rita Anne Weems in Jackson Heights, Queens, New York City, USA, on August 1, 1959. My father, Eddie Weems, fixed couches for Castro Convertible. My mother, Louisa Rosenthal Weems, was one of those hollowed-out blonde beauties who made their way to New York via Thereisenstadt and then a displaced person's camp. There are a lot of them still walking around. I see them on the subways now and then. But, in Jackson Heights where I grew up, they were a dime a dozen.

        My mother smoked four packages of Chesterfields a day and died of cancer when I was ten. All my memories of her are stained nicotine yellow, accompanied by a deep, painful hacking cough. Officially, I've given up on smoking. I rarely buy a pack. But some days I just do it. The privacy of a good smoke on a cold day. Feeling awkward around a table. Talking on the phone. Then, at night, I'll lie in bed clutching my breasts, my lungs, that hole in my chest where the burning smoke sits. My mind rolls over as I beg and beg for redemption.

        When I pray, I pray to the Jewish God. I pray to the

51

patriarchal God – not an energy or a spirit – but that old white man with a beard sitting up there deciding things. My mother prayed to him. My grandmother prayed to him and as far as I'm concerned, that is reason enough. We exist together in that moment of panic where my thoughts turn up to the sky.

My first job was cashier. Then I cleaned up a Catholic school cafeteria. All those girls in green plaid kilts with dusty white skin and matching white food. Instant mashed potatoes. Instant vanilla pudding. By senior year I started working at J. Chuckles on Forty-second Street in Manhattan. There I earned enough money to buy a camel's hair coat.

My mother, Louisa Rosenthal was born in Bremen and lost everything during the war. I, Rita, am named for her mother. My brother Howie is named for her father and my older brother Sam is named for her brother. Rest in peace. She married my dad, a Catholic. But my mother was a person who could not care about things like propriety. She just went through the motions. What could the neighbours do to her now?

My mother was the most beautiful woman in the world. She had that fragile, German, movie-star sensuality. She had blue eyes and soft lips. Her mouth was shapely. Her hair was fine and bright. But her eyes were nothing, flat. That worked though, for the completed beautiful victim look. I have a photograph of her in a suit with shoulder pads, when she first came to New York and was employed as a clerk at Woolworths. She had thick lipstick and pale empty eyes. On the way to work some fashion photographer saw her on the bus and invited her into his studio to take a few pictures. Her face was slightly twisted. She held a sultry cigarette.

'Your mother was like Marilyn Monroe,' my father said. 'A real doll.'

There are a few other photographs. Louisa and Eddie at Niagara Falls. Louisa and Eddie at Rockaway Beach. Louisa and Eddie eating a Kitchen Sink ice-cream sundae at Jahn's Ice Cream Parlour. The kids are in that one too. Me, age three, sitting on my father's lap. Sam, age seven, happy, benign, acting just the way kids are supposed to act. Howie, age ten, looking to the side at the wrong moment, ice cream all over his shirt.

Here is one of the classic Weems' family stories. It stars me, age two, sitting in the stroller at the German deli near the house where Louisa bought her teawurst.

'I'm not happy,' I reportedly announced in a booming bawl.

'Why not?' Mister Braunstein asked from behind the counter.

'I'm not happy,' I repeated, 'because my daddy isn't here.'

Where was he? Off in a car full of tools to some richer person's more expensive house in a better neighbourhood of Queens like Kew Gardens or Forest Hills or some place in the city or out on the island, the North Shore. He held the nails in his mouth and spit them out into place. He carried a hammer in the sling of his work pants thinking about the good old days in the army during the war. Mister Handsome G.I. Listening to the crap on the car radio. My dad knew all the songs.

Now, after a night of smoking, I lie in bed, terrified.

'What am I doing with a cigarette in my hand?' I ask myself stupidly. 'I've got to be out of my mind.'

These days everybody is dying. Not just my mother. There's no illusion left to let a person feel immune. Invincible is over.

I didn't get my mother's hair. Sam got it. Mine is blonde and brown, sign of mixed race. Howie looks even darker, real Black Irish, and that's fine. But this in-between kind of washed-out, blah sort of shut me down in the beauty department. I got blue eyes, true. But I also got blue skin, really pink nipples that look paraffin coated. No pubic hair on the insides of my thighs. Thank God. Whenever you see pubic hair in a movie or a magazine the girl's never got it down the insides of her thighs. But, in real life there are miles of it out there. There is wall to wall carpeting in every household in America. Some girls get embarrassed and some act like they never noticed. But there is a discrepancy between most thighs and the ideal ones. Mine are kind of ideal.

I grew up. I got jobs. I moved far from my destiny. No husband. No night school. No screaming kids in snow suits and strollers. No trappings. Not trapped.

My first lover was rough, knowing, leathery. She held my blue body. I was so young. I didn't know what love-making was. This woman was about forty, named Maria. She was sizeable, weighty, assuredly handsome. I had no expectations. I couldn't give anything back. As we were doing it, I just couldn't be free. Love-making seemed to revolve around the shifting of weight. It had to do with climbing onto Maria's body. Her whole skeleton was involved. But when she opened my lips and put her mouth on my clitoris I couldn't react. It was too specific. The rest of me felt lonely. I was seventeen. I had no extra flesh. Maria masturbated in front of me. I sat between her legs staring like it was a television set.

After that I just started talking, blabbing on and on. I told her everything I did all day and what I was expecting to do tomorrow. I told her about every song on the radio and which ones I liked, which ones did not deserve to be hits. I told her about the time, when my mother was sick, that some strange accented distant relative I'd never seen before or since took me to a store in Brooklyn to buy some clothes for the first day of school. I wore size 6X. I didn't understand why we had to go all the way to Brooklyn until we climbed up these shaky wooden stairs to the shop. The place was run by a group of friends who had been in the same concentration camp. All the clerks had numbers on their arms and screamed at each other like they were home in their kitchens.

The second time Maria picked me up from work and made me keep on all my clothes. She was smart. Passing her hands over my young breasts, there was no direct touching. No contact. That was the first time in my life that I ever felt sexy. That was the first time I ever felt that thing. Desire.

Further down, I thought. *Please put your hands further down.* I got angrier and angrier as her hands stayed the same.

'You've got to ask for it,' she whispered. She said it like a threat. 'You've got to ask for what you want.'

'Put your hands down there.'

'Down where?'

'In my pants.'

She lifted me onto her lap and fucked me fully clothed.

'*You* are a brave young girl,' she said. 'You're a darling girl. Keep your clothes on and it will always feel good.'

The next and final time together, it was my turn to touch. It was an inquiry. I hadn't yet discovered shame. But Maria's cunt didn't open to my fingers the way mine had to hers. That's when I realised how trust shows in sex. It has nothing to do with how they act or what they say. It shows physically. I learned, instinctively, the tell-tale signs.

Being a salesgirl was a trap. That was clear from the start. Dad's new girlfriend, Erica, worked in sales and she was obviously trapped. The staff at J. Chuckles were trapped. The manager was trapped. Even the customers were trapped by the lousy selection of over-priced clothes.

I knew that I was only seventeen. I knew I was young. This job was just a moment. It was just about saving up for a camel's hair coat. The coat was so dashing. It was substantial. It was something I had never seen before except on the back of a woman on line at Cinema One.

Saturday afternoons, after work, I went to Shield's Coffee Shop on Lexington Avenue and had an egg salad sandwich on rye. One dollar and five cents with a pickle on the side. I sat at the counter, exhausted, and stared out the window at the people on line at Cinema One. It was New York couples at Christmas time. The kind that went to foreign films. They had good taste. They weren't tacky little hitters from Queens. The girls in tight jeans and sparkle socks from my neighbourhood spent their whole lives smoking Marlboros in front of candy stores. Their boyfriends died in car accidents or never got rid of the drug habits they'd picked up in Vietnam. Those girls wore blue eye make-up. They listened to Elton John and Yes and Black Sabbath at parties. They listened to *Tommy* by The Who and Bachman-Turner *Overdrive*. They did Quaaludes with their older boyfriends and then eventually used needles and drank tequila right out of the bottle. They never saw foreign films. I hadn't either, but I would someday. That was the difference.

Outside the couples were standing in line. I ate my egg salad slowly, watching. Framed by the picture window was a distinguished older couple. The man wore a topcoat. His wife's hair was done. She linked her arm into his. They both looked ahead while discussing so they could watch and comment at the same time. Behind them stood a younger version. The woman's cheeks blushed pink between gold earrings. The younger guy wore a scarf and a jacket. His hair was long, hatless. Behind them stood two women, arms linked as well. They were engaged, laughed easily. One had to bend over slightly so the other could speak into her ear. And then something happened that changed my life forever. The two women kissed, romantically. The one nearest the window wore a camel's hair coat.

The next Saturday was Christmas Day. As soon as I could get out of the house, I took the Seven train into the city directly to Cinema One. I sat down in the virtually empty theatre and watched the same foreign film those two women had watched. It was called *Cries and Whispers*. In it, one woman touched another woman's face and kissed it. Another scene showed a different woman take out her breasts while a fourth laid her head on them. Then the first woman put a piece of glass in her vagina and rubbed the blood across her mouth. Throughout, a clock was ticking and people were whispering in Swedish. The subtitles said 'Forgive me'. I went downstairs into a stall in the ladies' bathroom and masturbated. Then I went up and watched it again.

That whole year my father and I were always fighting. If he told me to get out and never come back, I'd be hovering on the front stoop for hours screaming to get back in. If he put his foot down and told me I couldn't go out, I'd do it anyway by going down the fire escape. Our street, 82nd Street in Jackson Heights, was so quiet that me yelling or him yelling was enough for the whole neighbourhood to hear. After a few people started complaining my dad got into the habit of calling the local precinct as soon as we'd get into a fight.

'Officer,' he'd say into the telephone. 'We have a girl here, out of control.'

There were Spanish kids in Jackson Heights then but not so many as now. The Spanish and the whites never mixed. That really dates me. Out on the street were good girl German Jews coming home from their violin lessons and lots of Irish kids blaming themselves for everything starting at the age of twelve. I knew a girl who lived two apartments up from ours named Claudia Haas and she started out as a good girl but ended up as a tramp.

My father was a rough guy. He'd already chased Howie out of the apartment and off to California somewhere to find peace and fortune. His second girlfriend dumped him and it was taking dad longer than usual to find another one, which also put him in a foul mood. So, when he tossed me out for the fifteenth time, I shrugged it off and went to the candy store to buy a pack of Salem. There was Claudia Haas, tight jeans, tight V-neck short-sleeved sexy knit top. She was hanging out, a real hitter from Queens. She was drinking Mateus Rosé out of the bottle and listening to Seals and Crofts on WPLJ radio. The real truth is that Claudia Haas fell in love with me and I fell in love with her even though it wasn't possible on a warm Queens' night in 1975 because neither of us knew what a homosexual was. It wasn't a word that was bandied about the newspapers then as it is today. Even I, who had already experienced it, had never uttered the word. I had never conceptualised myself that way.

Claudia and I talked together until late that night. We sat on cars, smoked cigarettes, listened to Yes do 'Close To The Edge' and fell in love. Claudia's boyfriend wore his Vietnam army jacket, turned us on to Thai weed, drank beer, listened to Grand Funk Railroad, to WAR, to Average White Band and Janis Ian, to The Allman Brothers singing 'Whipping Post' live at The Fillmore East, to Carly Simon singing 'You're So Vain', to The Stones, Emerson Lake and Palmer, Acoustic Hot Tuna and The Dead. It was a different, stupid America. We hadn't yet given up trying to get over Vietnam. We revelled in our mediocrity. America wasn't nihilistic yet. We weren't all suffering.

That night, after partying, the sky was all mine, warm on my skin. I followed Claudia up to her parents' tiny apartment, like ours, four rooms smashed together into a purposeful square. Remove the walls and we're all head to toe, head to toe. Her mother had left the kitchen light on, illuminating a plate of *muhn kuchen* which we left, untouched on the rickety table.

'Come on,' Claudia whispered, leading me into the family bathroom where we spread out towels to lay stomach down on the cool tile floor.

'What's the green stuff?' I asked.

'Herbal Essence shampoo. Smell it.'

It smelled good. She had all kinds of things, special kinds of hair brushes and sponges, powder. I never learned how to use products. Didn't even know where to begin.

'Here, I'll brush your hair,' she said pulling it off the back of my neck.

'I looked at these at Field's,' I said. 'But I didn't know what they were.'

The brush felt so good against my neck, her hand there too.

Then we lay back on the floor, whispering, passing back cigarettes and blowing the smoke out through the open window.

'I'm going to Queens' College in the fall,' Claudia said, feet up, straight blonde hair cut back in a soft shag. 'What about you?'

'I kind of stopped going to school,' I said.

'What did your father say?'

'He hasn't mentioned it. I've been working at J. Chuckles, in the city. Is Queens' College really that great?'

'My sister's been there for three years. One more and then she'll move out. After that I've got the bedroom all to myself. I got wait-listed at two other places though, so the future is really unknown. Do you have a boyfriend?'

'Are you in love with Herbie?'

'Sure,' she said. 'You know what? He had this rubber last night. It said *Put a tiger in your dot dot dot.* Everything's fine except there's one thing about him that I really hate.'

'What's that?'

'When we're doing it, you know, balling? Sometimes he pushes my head down there because he wants a blow-job. I get really pissed off. *Don't tell me what to do.* I'm not some Vietnamese girl who has to do what he says. It's not nice.'

She rolled over on her side. I was used to the dark by now and the distant street lights started to work for me, started to glimmer like the light of the silvery moon, started to really light us up. Then Claudia started singing.

'*Du bist zaire ferucht. Du mus nach Berlin.*'

'What does that mean?'

'Don't you know German?'

'My mother forgot to teach us.'

'It means,' she said, brushing a piece of my hair back with her hand. 'You are so crazy, you must be from Berlin.'

I felt her touch me and I saw her do it as well. I saw a certain gentleness, a womanly softness as though reaching out to touch me was the most natural thing. It was *of course*. But somewhere, barely perceptible, I detected an excitement. Something crackling.

'*Fallink in luff again, nevah vanted to,*' she sang, taking my hand. '*Vat am I to do? Cahn't help it.*'

Silver Moon Bay

LISA ALTHER

'SO, CLASS, we still have a few minutes left before lunch,' said Mrs Murphy, glancing at the watch face pinned to her blouse by a tiny golden bow. 'Let's talk about the future. Tell me what you want to be when you grow up.'

As Stephanie watched her classmates raise their hands, she imagined herself dressed in chaps and a Stetson, riding a wild bull, or tending a patient on a pallet in a mud hut, wearing a pith helmet.

'I'm going to be a hunter,' announced Mike, who sat across the aisle from Stephanie.

'What about you, Stephanie?' asked Mrs Murphy.

Stephanie looked up dreamily. 'I want to be a hero.'

Her classmates turned around to look at her.

'Don't be dumb,' muttered Mike. 'Girls can't be heroes.'

Stephanie regarded him coolly, picturing herself in a visored helmet and armour, waving a banner studded with fleurs-de-lis. Or sitting in a cockpit wearing a jump suit and a leather cap with fur ear flaps.

* * *

Stephanie and her girlfriends were weaving dandelions into tiaras when the boys came crawling across the playground, shirtless, faces painted with lipstick, crow feathers taped to their temples. Seeing the boys slithering towards them like evil snakes, the girls began to scream.

Removing her circlet of flowers, Stephanie stood up and marched over to the prostrate boys. 'Stop it right now.'

Mike stood up and glared at her as his braves scrambled to their feet.

'Go away and leave us alone, creep,' said Stephanie.

'You think you're so great,' said Mike, 'but everybody knows your old lady's a witch.'

Stephanie opened her mouth to reply, but closed it again.

'She swims with the lake monster on full moon nights,' called Mike as the boys turned to leave.

Lance, Mike's best friend, added, 'My dad says that the bodies of people who drown in Silver Moon Bay are never found because your mother calls the monster to come carry them down into its underwater cave.'

Stephanie stared at the ground saying nothing.

'Well, for goodness sakes, Stephanie, why did you make them leave?' hissed Missy, the girl who had been screaming most loudly. 'What in the world is wrong with you?'

After school Stephanie headed down the dirt road toward the lake through a dense evergreen forest, swinging her canvas book bag. Her sheepdog Otto was trotting next to her. At the roadside, stretched between two stalks of purple wild aster, she spotted a shimmering spider web. In the centre an orange and black Monarch butterfly was struggling weakly while a metallic green spider with a crimson belly crossed the web like a sailor scaling a rigging. Stephanie squatted down and plucked the butterfly from the sticky web with two fingers. The spider watched indignantly while the butterfly lifted off from her palm and was carried towards the treetops on a breeze off the lake.

Down by the rocky shore Stephanie could see the wooden cottage where she lived with her mother. On the far side of the water, high forested mountains formed the horizon. Lush gardens of flowers and vegetables surrounded the house. Stephanie's mother stood in one, harvesting corn. She paused to shield her eyes against the sun. Spotting Stephanie descending the ridge, she waved.

Stephanie sat on a rock ledge that had been scored by a glacier thousands of years earlier and watched her mother tying corn stalks into shocks. Her mother kept glancing at her, concerned by her troubled silence.

'At school today some boys said you're a witch,' Stephanie finally said.

'Oh?' Her mother paused to look at her.

'Is that why Dad left?'

Her mother straightened up and kneaded the small of her back. 'Your father left because he wants to live in town near his paper mill. And I wanted to stay here by the lake.'

'Do you really swim with the monster at night?'

Her mother smiled. 'No. But I've seen it.'

'Really? What did it look like?'

'Well, it was nearly dark and the bay was like glass. I heard some waves breaking on the rocks, so I went down to the lake. I could see a V-shaped wake moving along the shore. When it reached me, I realised it was a giant snake, sidewinding through the water. It had several flowing black humps that glistened in the twilight. As it passed me, it lifted its head and seemed to look right at me with its yellow eyes. The head was shaped like a horse's, and the neck was long and curved, like the trunk of a sapling in a windstorm.'

'Were you afraid?'

'No. It's never harmed anyone. In fact, I was flattered that it trusted me enough to show itself to me. Hunters hide along the shore trying to shoot it.'

'Why?'

'The chamber of commerce in town has offered a reward. The rumours about a lake monster scare away tourists. But a stuffed one on display would attract them.'

'Could I see it sometime?' asked Stephanie, throwing a stick across the grass for Otto to retrieve.

'Maybe. If you want to enough. It's up to the monster, not me.'

After finishing the supper dishes that night, Stephanie sat down at the kitchen table beside the cast iron cook stove to read her horoscope in the evening paper: 'You are one of the pure at heart. You cannot fail.'

Laying the paper aside, she went outside. The full moon was casting a shimmering silver disc on the water. Sitting down with Otto on a rock, she gazed across the bay to the undulating mountains. Softly she chanted, 'Monster, monster, here's my order: take me with you underwater.'

Standing in the forest beside a birch tree, Stephanie touched with her fingertips a heart carved into the flaky white bark, which encircled the words 'Mike + Steph'. When they had entered high school, Mike had decided Stephanie was the girl for him, and she hadn't been able to dissuade him. Now that they had graduated, he had decided they were going to get married.

'How would you like it if someone carved a heart on your thigh?' she asked him.

'But I love you, Stephanie, and I want the world to know it,' he insisted. 'I'm going to kill the lake monster, and use the prize money to build a beautiful house for you and our babies.'

'I've told you a thousand times that I'm not marrying anyone,' she muttered. Least of all you, she thought.

'What *are* you going to do then?' Mike asked irritably.

'I'm going to be a hero.'

'Grow up, Stephanie. You're not a child anymore.' He stomped off into the forest.

'Why should I grow up?' wondered Stephanie as she walked down the hill towards home. She couldn't see anything about adult life to recommend it. The boys she'd gone to school with now spent their weekdays cutting down the forest for her father's paper mill and their weekends killing small animals in the woods. The girls were marrying these boys and having babies and watching soap operas and getting divorced.

Wandering along the lake shore, she bent down to pick up a flopping perch that had beached itself. After gently stroking its florescent indigo polka dots, she tossed it back into the water. Watching it glide away with a grateful flick of its tail, she murmured, 'Monster, monster, please be true: take me down below with you.'

Towards midnight Otto began growling on the hooked rug beside Stephanie's bed. Jerking awake, she rolled out from under the covers and threw on her robe. She and Otto raced out of the house and across the lawn. Waves were crashing on the rock ledges, but the bay was otherwise still and silver in the moonlight. Otto was barking frantically. Watching the waves pound the shore, Stephanie pleaded, 'Monster, monster, please come back. I'd follow you, but I lack the knack.'

Standing by the desk in her father's office the next afternoon, Stephanie looked out the window to a mountain of logs over which steel cranes were hovering like giant praying mantises.

'. . . So I was thinking,' her father was saying as he stretched in his swivel chair and clasped his hands behind his head with his elbows extended, 'that you could move into town and work here with me to learn the ropes. And one day this could all be yours.'

As Stephanie watched a crane seize a huge tree trunk in its jaws and lower it onto a flatbed railroad car, she thought this over. She had hoped to be a hero, but opportunities for heroism seemed in short supply. At least she could do something useful while she awaited her moment.

* * *

Strolling around her father's condominium that evening, Stephanie inspected all his gadgets – a television with a screen that filled one wall, a stereo as complicated as a jetliner dashboard, a washing machine that had to be programmed like a weapons' system. Maybe it wouldn't be so bad to live with all this luxury, after nearly two decades in a cottage by the lake with oil lamps and a cookstove and dried herbs hanging from the beams? She sat down at the glass dining table where her father was spooning Chinese take-out onto black enamel plates.

As she tried to manoeuvre chopsticks, her father said, 'At least consider it, Stephanie. You're an adult now. You've got to do *something*. You can't just vegetate there by the lake forever.'

'Okay, Dad. I'll think it over.' Picking up a fortune cookie, she broke it open. The message read, 'Stay true to your dreams and ideals.'

Lying in the giant king-sized bed in her father's guest room the next morning, Stephanie could see the view through the floor-to-ceiling window, which the dark had concealed the previous evening. The river below was frothing with foam. Dead fish were floating atop the surface and littering the shores. The forest on the far bank had been reduced to stumps. Huge gullies had formed. A giant pipe from the mill was gushing waste into the water. Stephanie lay there staring at this scene for a long time.

'Stephanie and I need to talk,' her father was telling her mother as they stood outside her house by the lakeshore.

'I'm afraid she refuses to see you, Jason. She's very upset.'

Jason turned to walk back to his Acura. 'It's your fault, Iris. You've put all these bleeding heart ideas into her head. Ask her what pays for you two to live so comfortably, if not profits from my mill. Ask her where the paper in those books she loves to read comes from.'

That afternoon as Stephanie listlessly tied corn stalks into a shock, she asked. 'Don't you ever get bored with this, Mother? Plant, weed, pick, can. Sometimes you don't even pick: plant, weed, rot. Plant, weed, rot. Year after year. It's pointless.'

Iris gave her daughter a long-suffering look. 'You need to find something to do with yourself, dear.'

'Like what, for instance?' Stephanie snarled. Hurling the corn stalks into the dirt, she marched toward the house.

As she placed a tea bag in a mug and waited for the water to boil on the cookstove, she read the tag: 'Your future is as boundless as the lofty heavens.'

'Yeah, right,' she muttered. 'Tell me about it.'

Duck blinds camouflaged with evergreen boughs dotted Silver Moon Bay. Rifle barrels glinted behind them in the sun. As Vs of southbound ducks and geese passed overhead, the rifles blasted, bringing birds spiralling to the lake surface, where retrievers seized them in their jaws and carried them to their masters.

Stephanie, Otto at her side, was rescuing a crimson dragonfly from drowning when Mike rowed up in his inflatable raft. He was wearing army camouflage, and his face was blackened with burnt cork. He hopped ashore carrying a rifle and a bunch of dead ducks, which he thrust at Stephanie. 'For dinner tonight for you and your mother,' he explained.

'You're very kind, but no thanks.' As Stephanie handed them back, she thought that she'd rather starve first.

'Changed your mind yet about marrying me, Steph?' he asked with his most winning smile. 'You wouldn't be sorry. I'd take good care of you. I'm cutting trees for your father now. I get a pay cheque every week.'

Stephanie shook her head. 'Please just give it a rest, Mike. I'm not going to change my mind.'

'Is there someone else?' he asked grimly. 'Just tell me the truth.'

'There's no one else,' she assured him sadly.

After he left, Stephanie sat on the rocks in the sunset with Otto, gazing across the crimson lake. 'Monster, monster, pass this way,' she chanted. 'I wait for you both night and day.'

Jumping up impatiently, she threw off her jeans and flannel shirt and pulled on her wet suit. Shoving her windsurfer into the water, she climbed aboard. When Otto tried to join her, she pushed him ashore with her foot. 'I'm sorry, Otto,' she said, 'but you can't come. I've got to go alone and find the monster.'

A gust filled her turquoise and yellow sail, carrying her towards the forested mountains on the far shore, behind which the fiery orange sun was sinking. She could hear Otto howling mournfully from the rocks. A strong north wind swept down the lake. Although she fought it with all her strength, as though arm wrestling the wind, it finally forced the mast down to the surface of the lake, so that Stephanie somersaulted across the board and into the freezing water.

Bobbing beside her wilted sail in the gathering dusk, trying to summon enough strength to climb back onto the board, Stephanie was amazed to find herself suddenly rising high up into the air. Looking down, she discovered she was riding the back of a glistening serpent. Smiling, she wrapped her arms around its arching neck as it dove beneath the waves.

The monster carried Stephanie deeper and deeper, to darker and darker depths. On all sides giant fish were grazing and swaying. The lake floor consisted of mountains and valleys identical to those on land, forested with dark slimy seaweed. As the serpent glided through gaping jaws of stone into a dim grotto, Stephanie lost consciousness.

Sitting up, Stephanie found herself in a vast above-ground cavern surrounded by monsters of all sizes. Several storeys of caves had been hollowed into the encircling walls, which were decorated with colourful murals featuring monsters engaged in unidentifiable activities.

'Don't be alarmed,' said the monster whose back she had ridden. 'You're among friends.'

'You talk?' gasped Stephanie.

'Not among ourselves. But with humans, yes.'

'Where am I?'

'In the middle of the mountain across the lake from your mother's house.'

The monster picked Stephanie up gently in its fins and carried her to a small cave.

'Why have you brought me here?' she asked uneasily.

'We can talk about that later. First get some rest.'

As it laid her carefully into a bowl in the rock floor, Stephanie asked herself why she wasn't afraid to be trapped in a cave full of hideous mammoth serpents with fins.

Several monsters including Stephanie's were coiled in a circle on couches of stone with Stephanie in the middle.

'Let me get this straight,' she was saying. 'Silver Moon Bay connects through underground rivers and seas with bodies of water all over the world?'

Her monster nodded.

'And all the mountains on earth are hollow and full of creatures like you. But how did you get here in the first place?'

The silence was broken only by water lapping the stone ramp that descended from this reception hall to lake level.

'What's going on? Did I say something wrong?' Stephanie asked her monster.

'I'm translating what you said. From speech into thought.'

The silence dragged on for quite a while.

'I've been told to answer you,' her monster finally said. 'Relax, because it's a long story: 230 million years ago our forebears lived on land, eating small plants and leaves. Vicious predators began to chase and murder and eat us. So, reversing evolution, we returned to the water, where we gradually developed breathing tubes and learned to eat kelp and plankton. Eventually we discovered underwater caverns and made our homes there.

'Then, 65 million years ago, an asteroid from outer space socked the earth, igniting forest fires, causing volcanos to erupt, and sweeping the seacoasts with tidal waves. In the endless winter caused by all the dust and smoke we watched our old enemies on land sicken and die from cold and starvation. But we were safe deep in our underwater caves, still able to scavenge enough marine vegetation to survive. We were sad about the devastation, but hopeful for a peaceful new world free of our ancient predators.

'Eventually the land came alive again, this time with mammals. The tiny land reptiles that had survived evolved wings and feathers and took to the skies. Unfortunately, our dream of a harmonious world was not to be. Soon mammals reigned. Periodically glaciers would creep across the land, destroying them. But always a few remained to continue the killing...'

'I guess I want to go home now,' murmured Stephanie, not pleased to be a mammal. 'Okay?' She was trying to figure out whether she was a prisoner or a guest.

The monsters just sat there in an irritating telepathic silence.

'I've been instructed to give you a tour of our cavern first, if you like,' said Stephanie's monster.

'So heat rises from the earth's core to warm our cavern,' Stephanie's monster explained as it and Stephanie inspected an elaborate network of stone shafts and duct-work.

'What's your name anyway?' asked Stephanie.

The monster looked blank. 'We don't really have names. Since we don't use words, we ... sense each other's essence. It's hard to explain.'

'How do you tell each other apart?'

'Most of the time we don't need to tell each other apart. Besides, words can lie. So we watch each other's behaviour and listen to each other's hearts.'

'I don't get it.'

'Why don't you just call me Dion?'

'Why Dion?'

The monster twisted and boogyed, a dreamy look in its yellow eyes. 'I used to love those songs by Dion and the Belmonts that teenagers played in their powerboats back in the sixties. Do you know 'Runaround Sue'?'

'So are you male or female or what?'

'We're all everything.' Dion's green face blushed.

'So you're bisexual?'

'Not exactly.' Clearly wanting to change the subject, Dion pointed to a nearby canal. 'If you swim down that river, you come to the underground sea where we hold our international reunions and conventions. And from there you can take a river that runs into the Atlantic.'

Stephanie looked at Dion incredulously.

'. . . So each of us lives alone in one of these cells every now and then. To renew our link with the cosmos,' said Dion, standing with Stephanie before some caves deep in the interior of the cavern. 'When you're alone, you remember what's really important.'

'And what's that?' asked Stephanie.

Dion grimaced. 'I don't know how to translate it into words. You'll have to try it for yourself sometime.'

'Thanks all the same, but I'd like to go home now.'

'I'll take you home whenever you want, Stephanie,' said Dion sadly. 'It's not our way to force anyone to do anything. But I was hoping you might want to stay for the dance tonight.'

'Dance?'

'We have all kinds of entertainment down here. When you don't have wars, you have time and energy for other things. Like feeding and sheltering everyone, and enjoying the new babies, and singing and dancing and painting and making up stories.'

'You don't have wars?'

'We've watched too many mammal wars on Silver Moon Bay to want any of our own. The Iroquoise-Algonquin War, the French and Indian War, the American Revolution, the War of 1812. Each of your wars is exactly the same. We can't understand why you don't get bored with them. The sky turns murky orange from the conflagrations. The lake water becomes streaked with gore. Mangled corpses sink to the bottom, where the giant fish rip them to pieces. We do what we can to help the women and children, the old and the sick, carrying them to shore after boats sink, hiding them in caves when they're being pursued. But we rarely save the soldiers and sailors, because it's best for all of us if the aggressive destroy each other. Sometimes our young who yearn to be warriors themselves go up and turn over a gunboat or two, just so they can see how silly and cruel it is.'

'I'm so ashamed,' murmured Stephanie.

'I can imagine,' said Dion gently. 'It's not a pretty picture. We've existed for 230 million years with brains the size of walnuts. Humans with their grapefruit brains are going to self-destruct after only three million years. But the vicious and greedy species always do in time. We've watched many come and go.'

'If you're so perfect, how come you're extinct?' asked Stephanie, suddenly annoyed by this arrogant reptile.

'Do we look extinct?'

'Forgive me,' said Stephanie. 'It's just so embarrassing being a human.'

'Why have you brought me here, Dion?' Stephanie asked that night as they watched some sinuous monsters perform an elaborate folk dance that wove a beautiful pattern of interlacing arabesques.

'Sometimes we show ourselves to humans we hope can accept us without reaching for their rifles. And after all, we've been in touch with you for years.'

'You have?'

'Where do you think all those messages on your tea bags and in your fortune cookies came from? And haven't you been sitting by the lake shore calling us for years?'

'But how . . . ?'

'You may need us, Stephanie. But we need you too. The chemicals from your father's mill are poisoning the lake. Some of our babies have already been born with deformities. In time we'll all be dead. And so will you.'

'I never realised. But of course I'll go back home and talk with him.'

As she and Dion stood before the doorway to her guest cave after the dance, Stephanie wondered if she'd begun to fall in love with Dion. But since she'd never been in love before, she wasn't sure. Was it possible that if she kissed Dion, the monster would turn into a prince? Or a princess?

'Thank you for a memorable day, Dion.' She put a hand on either side of the monster's horse-like head and gently kissed the narrow green lips.

Stephanie was transformed into a monster.

Later that night Stephanie and Dion were lying cradled in each other's fins in the guest cave, coils plaited together. Now that she too was a monster, Stephanie could understand Dion's thoughts. 'I've loved you for years,' Dion was thinking. 'I used to watch from the marsh as you rescued drowning dragonflies. And I'd go mad when you'd call for us. Sometimes emissaries from down here had to come persuade me to go home before I froze to death in the mud.'

Dion sat up abruptly.

'What's wrong, darling?' thought Stephanie.

'The mammal alarm has gone off. Humans are trying to enter the cavern.'

Dion and several other monsters gathered in the entrance hall to pull on rubber masks of Stalin, Hitler, Mao, the Ayatollah... One by one they slithered down the stone ramp into the water. Once assembled into a flotilla, they swam to the cave mouth. A team of scuba divers was approaching. After turning their flashlights onto the monsters in their masks, the divers whirled around and fled in terror, frog fins churning.

'You've got to stop this, Iris,' Jason was telling Stephanie's mother as she wept beside her tangled neglected gardens. 'You've done nothing but cry ever since Stephanie disappeared.'

'She's still alive. I can feel it, Jason. Something awful has happened to her.'

'What more can I do? I've got boats sweeping the lake with sonar nets. We've baited huge hooks with calves' heads. Remote-control vehicles are searching the lake floor. Mike's assembled a team of scuba divers. Rescue squads are scouring the forests. If Stephanie is anywhere in this state, we'll find her.'

Mike's powerboat careened ashore and he jumped out in his wet suit. 'We've found the monster cave, sir. It's full of world dictators. I'd like your permission to bomb it.'

'How will that help to find my daughter?' asked Jason.

Mike drew Jason aside so Iris couldn't hear. His eyes were full of tears. 'If Stephanie is down there, sir, she's dead. I'm sorry to put it so bluntly, but that cave is flooded with water. I loved Stephanie. I was going to marry her. I hate those creatures for robbing me of my bride. I want them dead. Afterwards, we can search their cave and maybe bring her body home. If they haven't already ripped it apart and devoured it.'

'Stephanie, your father is going to destroy us – with his bombs or with his poison,' Dion was thinking. 'If you love us, please go back and talk to him.' The monster council behind him was nodding urgent agreement.

'But you love me too, Dion,' Stephanie thought. 'Or at least that's what you say. So how can you send me away?'

Dion looked acutely embarrassed. The others eyed the young monster indulgently.

'All right. I'll go,' Stephanie thought reluctantly. 'But only if you'll come too, Dion. If I can turn into a reptile from love of you, surely you can become human from love of me?'

One of the monster elders thought, 'But this is impossible, Stephanie. Your "Dion" would become instantly insane from having to choose whether to be male or female.'

Stephanie began to weep. 'But I want to stay here with all of you. I feel at home here. I never have up there.'

'This is your chance to be a real hero,' replied the elder. 'You can save us. If you stay here, we'll all die. But we would never take you back to land unless you chose to go.'

'If I go talk to my father, can I return here afterwards?'

'Why not go home for part of each year to keep your humans happy. Then return to us for the rest of the year.'

'It's a deal.' Stephanie swayed her long neck over to kiss Dion with her thin green lips.

Stephanie in human form climbed off Dion's back by the lake shore. As Dion dove beneath the surface, she waved sadly.

When she reached her mother's house, Otto hurled himself at her, barking joyously.

'Where have you been, dear?' her mother asked from the doorway, looking haggard and annoyed. 'Are you all right? We've been so worried.'

'I'm really sorry, Mom, but it's something I had to do,' replied Stephanie. 'I'm in love for the first time in my life, but I don't want to say any more about it.'

'. . . So what you do here, Dad, affects the water all over the 'globe,' Stephanie was telling her father, who was sitting behind the huge walnut desk in his office at the mill. 'What about if I work with you to find some solutions?'

'I don't know,' he said glumly. 'It sounds like one of your mother's bizarre holistic hallucinations. But I'll think it over. Meanwhile, we need to discuss your morals. Your mother tells me ...'

'Oh come on, Daddy. I know there must have been a time when you were young and in love. Surely you weren't always such a grumpy old drag?'

He smiled reluctantly. 'Is it Mike?'

'Mike? Mike's a maniac. He's going around town telling people he found a cave full of world dictators at the bottom of the lake. I think you ought to send him away somewhere for a rest cure.'

'He does seem to have lost it. Maybe I'd better transfer him to the New Jersey plant for a few years.'

'Good idea.'

'You're so pleasant and helpful these days,' Iris was saying to Stephanie as they worked together trying to get the gardens back in shape. 'Being in love clearly agrees with you. Who is it?'

'Let's just say I'm in love with the lake monster.'

Iris laughed. 'All right. I know when I'm being told to mind my own business.'

Stephanie waved surreptitiously to Dion, who was lying in the mud in the marsh watching her pull weeds.

As an autumn wind whirled scarlet leaves off the sugar maple trees in the forest, Stephanie and Otto climbed from the rock ledge along the lake onto Dion's back. Clinging to the arching neck, they rode across the bay towards the far mountains, along the silver pathway paved by the full harvest moon overhead.

The Ladies are Upstairs

MERLE COLLINS

MOONLIGHT TONIGHT. Long time, now, we would be outside singing and dancing.

Tantie Mary, thread the needle
Ring ting, thread the needle. Tantie Mary...

Long time.

Moonlight tonight. After one time is another. I can't hear no little child voice outside tonight. And me self, I inside here sitting down waiting for them to bring on 'The Young and the Restless'. And me grand-daughter stand up out there on the step looking up at the sky. Moon full, yes, she say, as if she surprise. Is like that. When night dark, you waiting and hoping for moonlight. And when it come, so swift and so sudden, it surprise you. You even forget what darkness was like. But is a strange thing; when darkness there, you never forget what moonlight was like.

Moonlight tonight. And where I sit down here with the television watching me, what you think I remember? Miss Mary. Look at that, eh! After all these years! I talking to meself? Well, with these years on me head, is all right to talk to meself sometimes. Seventy years I making this christmas. Is to be expected. But is something I remember. Go back and watch you moonlight. All right, then, let me tell you if you want to know. It look like they push back this programme well late tonight. Leave the door. Leave it open.

Is Miss Mary I remember, this moonlight night. Miss Mary and Belmont river. I was walking home from by your aunt in La Poterie. I stay late. Moon full and lighting up the road bright like tonight. And reach I reach by Belmont bridge, what you think I see in the river? I shouldn't say what, non. Shouldn't call people what no matter the state that they reach. Is who you think I see in the river? Miss Mary. Sitting down on river stone in the middle of the river. To understand what a shock that was you have to know who Miss Mary really was, and the height these people was in the place. You don't remember I tell you about Miss Mary long time? You probably forget.

But anyway, see I see the figure in the river, I say, Lord have is mercy! La diablesse! What you closing the door for? Big hard-back woman like you, still fraid la diablesse story? And is not even la diablesse story. I thinking, moonlight and la diablesse combing she hair on river-stone like mermaid. I stand up there paralyse. Ready to run. Then la diablesse stretch out she two hand wide and turn round. Miss Mary, yes. Imagine! After one time is another.

Miss Mary and she sisters grow up pectus, pectus in the house on the hill. Was a house everybody in the village could see. Bigger than everybody own. The house on the hill. Fly couldn't touch them. Me sister used to say they messin ice cream. If wind blow too hard and ruffle them little bit, Madam, their mother, would employ the whole district to take care of them. Look at that, eh! And their father was a very drastic man. A big shot; a big jefe and he never had a pleasant word for nobody. And those little girls, Miss Mary and she sisters, fly couldn't touch them, I tell you.

I call out. 'Miss Mary! Miss Mary!' She turn round. Stand up there rocking on the river stone and waving. 'Bella!' she shouting. 'Bella!' Like me is a long-lost friend. I don't want to laugh, non, child, but after one time is another in truth!

I telling you like this, it sounding simple, but you could never imagine what it was like in those days. I remember one time, after me mother find a little work for me in the house, because she used to work domestic there for a long time, you know, well, she come and find this little work for me in the house. I used to go there mostly weekends, and sometimes Monday if they had a lot of washing, and sometimes Friday, for cleaning and dusting and so. I remember one time, a lady pass selling fish. Was jacks.

Madam, Miss Margaret mother, was upstairs. I know Madam did say she would like to buy some jacks. The lady was down by the gate. I hear the dogs barking and when I look out, the yard-boy was holding them back and talking to the lady with her basket on the other side of the gate. So I tell Cook. And she tell me to go and ask Madam. And same time she push the window and call out to the yard-boy, and he secure the dogs and open the gate for the lady. I run inside and call out to Madam upstairs.

'Madam! Madam! A lady in the yard with jacks.'

Well! Madam appear at the top of the stairs. Is as if I could see her now. Standing up there in a kind of gold colour dress with she hand resting on the bannister. 'What's that, child? Why are you shouting? Haven't I told you not to shout?'

'Sorry, Madam. Is a lady, Madam. A lady in the yard with jacks, and Cook say to ask you if you want.'

And you should see the Madam. She raise both hands and put on her waist. 'A LADY in the yard with jacks?' she ask me. And then she lift one hand and point back upstairs, back into the bedrooms and the sitting room and so up there. 'The

LADIES are upstairs.' You laughing? The ladies are upstairs, she tell me, oui. So you understand what I saying about Miss Mary in the river.

Is a good thing Madam dead and gone by the time Miss Mary reach river stone. People say was always a sadness that the family never have any boy-children inside, to carry on the name, but God must be know what he do. Must be better so.

Was Grenada white, you know. The Boss-Man was black. Why you surprise? I tell you was the Boss-Man. I didn't tell you was white. His family was black people of substance from time. People with property. I can't say where the money come from, but wasn't poor people. And then he come and marry this white lady. Well, they say she had black in her, but when you watch her, is white lady you seeing. Was family with name, you know, but without the means. So the two put together come and solve the problem. His family had three boys. And all make good marriage. None of them marry Black.

And then, I don't know how it happen, but people say he come and lose his money. Everything, all property they had, had to sell to pay debt. One of his brothers buy the house so they could get it to stay, but they couldn't even afford to keep it up like before. Grass start to grow high, high in the yard. Nobody working for them no more. Then the Boss-Man come and dead, one lick. The big daughter, Miss Mavis, go and work somewhere in town and take the mother with her. I hear the Madam waste away. Dead talking stupidness, not knowing nobody, thank God, because by this time Miss Mary self start roaming the street. Miss Mavis went away, in the end, to England or somewhere, and you know, I don't even know what happen to the other one. I don't know. But when I come back from Maturín in Venezuela and see Miss Mary walking the streets, I couldn't believe. I just couldn't believe was the same little girl I did know.

My mother had a word she use to say, 'How have the mighty fallen!' And that was it, for true! How have the mighty fallen! The boys in the area used to hold Miss Mary hand and drag her in bush all over the place, do what they want with her. And everybody still saying 'Miss Mary', you know, from habit, but doing just what they want with her. And then the children start to call her Miss Mary Zagzo, because she was so thin and so wasted. And was to hear those worthless boys shouting out, 'Miss Mary Zagzo, you want to go under the cocoa?' And you know, jefe how they was in their day, I could never rejoice, because who know what life have in store? I was never high like them, is true, but still sometimes I find myself thinking, there but for the grace of God! Miss Mary! I used to watch those boys how they dragging her and think was the ending of the world!

That night, eh, child, I sit down on the river-bank and call out to Miss Mary to tell her come out of the river. The thing is, you never know when the river could come down all of a sudden, because rain might well be falling in the mountain. Push the door close little bit, you hear, child. The breeze blowing cold. Miss Mary, eh! Dancing on the river stone down there and looking up at me and laughing. 'Bella!' she saying. 'Is not Bella, then? Come here, Bella.' And meself calling, 'Come, Miss Mary. Come out of the river.' And she? Looking down at the river, stretching out her hands and turning right around, looking up at me and laughing.

'I see you come back to Grenada and build block house, Bella,' she saying. 'You know the song, Bella?' she shouting.

'What song, Miss Mary? Careful, Miss Mary. You will fall in the river, you know.'

'The song about

> *those far-away places*
> *where the strange calling names*
> *Far away, over the sea.'*

And she giggling. Was a song I grow up hearing. A song

people used to sing. And I used to hear it in their house a lot, when I working there, because in those days, was Boss-Man alone really had radio in the area. Sometimes he used to play it loud enough, too, when the good mood take him, so people could hear it from the road below.

> *'Those far-away places*
> *where the strange calling names*
> *Far away, over the sea.'*

So I tell Miss Mary yes, I know the song. And she say, 'Well, look you go away and come back to build block house. I want to go to one of those far-away places, Bella, those far-away places, where the strange calling names.'

And she throw back her head and laughing so much, that eventually I just leave her there, balancing on the river stone in the moonlight, and singing

> *'Those far-away places*
> *where the strange calling names*
> *Far away, over the sea.'*

Moonlight tonight, eh. And not one little one outside singing like in long time days. Even not so long ago the children used to be out there singing. You know the one that go *Tantie Mary, thread the needle* . . .

Yes. That is it.

> *Ring ting, thread the needle.*
> *Thread the needle, let me see you* . . .

Go and watch you moonlight, you hear, child. It don't look like 'The Young and the Restless' coming on tonight. Look how after all of these years I remember Miss Mary in the river, eh! After all these years!

Siren Song

SARA MAITLAND

Come, sailor, I am your dreaming;
long voyaging on icy seas
leads to the white haven of my arms.

IT IS never silent on the sea coast. There is always, even in a flat calm, the whispered sound of the smallest waves licking the silvered sand of the beach, tongueing the face of the rocks, and the soft sigh of the sand as each wave retreats and a few grains are carried down with it, reluctantly, inexorably.

It is never silent on the sea coast, but sometimes, at night, in the summer months, there can be a fleeting moment of something sweeter than silence: a magical hush. The soft irregular rhythms of that continuous rise and fall, rise and fall, rise and fall, rise and fall, become so monotonous, so expected and so gentle, that they fit perfectly to heartbeat and to breathing; out on the sea-way there is a slow roll of water, a gentle heave and a flowing gleam of phosphorescence, and we know a porpoise is passing on its long travels.

In that moment, just occasionally, but worth the long

expectancy, the moon rises, full, round, silver, and lays her swathe of white light across the barely shifting waters, and the twin points of light on the facing slope of each slow lift of water dance in delight. The moon at her full puts out the stars around her, but in compensation lays these dancing stars on the sea itself. The air is balmy, heavy, scented with summer and with seaweed. And if on such nights as these, we lay our hands or bare arms so that the moonbeams fall on them, we can feel – attenuated, fragile, delicate – the warmth of the sun, kissing his virgin sister, and letting the last reverberation of his power refracted from her across the wide spaces, caress us in the darkness of the night.

When the white lady rides her pathway on the sea, when all else is still, when the waves have sunk to this sparkling, dancing murmur, then we rise from our nest and preen ourselves, preparing ourselves as the young bride does for her beloved and with an excitement that is not altogether different although we wish that it were.

We wait.

It is our destiny to wait, but we chose that destiny and so our waiting is not the anxious wonderings of the sailor's beloved in the noisy harbours north of us. Will he come? Will he come on this light breeze, bending his back to the drum beat and pulling wearily? Or on another, on the shoulder of a storm? Or out of the sunset boldly, with the sails set, filled with a home wind and a golden light? Will he come today? Tomorrow? Will he ever come again?

Our waiting is not like that. It is a long calm waiting and we are always ready when he comes.

We wait.

And so, when those other three sisters, the Fates, have spun a sailor's life-thread so thin and taut that it can be spun no further, then far away a new rhythm begins, so gentle and distant that it is hard to be certain, although we are certain.

More a movement on the surface of the water than a sound, but the feathers, the hairs – both – on our necks rise sensitive to his coming and we smile a little at each other and preen.

And carried on the calm night the sound of his coming takes shape. The slow drum beat counts out the strokes. The cry of the helmsman in the stern is borne across the surface of the water to our longing ears. 'In,' he cries, '... and out. In – two, three; out – two three.' The oars hit the surface together as he calls them; the drum and the oars and the strong rich voice of the helmsman. 'In ... out ... in ... out.'

They are freemen who row such a ship, for we do not hear the harsh sound of the lash; a dark arhythmic note, joyless and painful, with which we have no business, no concern. As soon as we hear the coming of the ship clearly, we draw breath and we strike the chord and we sing, so that our singing runs out along the pathway that the moon is making, towards the approaching ship. And the sweetness of our singing in the moonlight is what all men dream of.

The sound of our music comes to them first so gentle and distant that it is hard to be certain. Perhaps it is just the wishes of tired men rowing southwards through a calm night. We sing and the sound of our music swelling in the darkness becomes unmistakeable, mysterious, desirable. The sweetness of our singing makes it so that each man believes we sing to him, for him alone. He does not see the rapt face of his companion on the rowing bench; he does not notice that he too has raised his head from the low easy slouch of the practised rower and has thrown it back, harkening to the music that is coming across the moonlight as his mother used to come when he cried in the night.

> Come sailor, I am your dreaming;
> long voyaging on icy seas
> leads to the white haven of my arms.
> Come, sailor.

At home your mother weeps for you;
She begs Athene, lover of brave men,
to bring her boy child home to her.
The candle she has lit for you
dims in the twin flames of my eyes.
Put out her candle, sailor,
and I will give you a place for each strong limb.

We sing to each man alone and what we sing is what he dreams.

If he dreams of his mother, he will hear her voice in our song, he will see her sad patient waiting and her joy at his coming.

If he dreams of power and glory, swords will flash in the moonlight, like hot day, and chariot wheels will throw up the spray of the sea like dust, and the crown of laurel will glimmer on his brow.

If he dreams of wealth, Hera, Queen of Olympus, will descend and give him the jewels from her peacocks' tails and the golden apples from the islands beyond the uttermost west.

If he dreams of poetry, the moon herself, Artemis the pure, will offer to teach him the music of the spheres, and he will hear the roar of applause in the amphitheatre, taste the pride of his city and the immortality of his name.

If he dreams of the gods, Poseidon will rise glorious on the wave-crest and greet him as lover and as friend; the dark voice of the sibyl will speak of the great mysteries in the cave and he will understand her as though she were his own chattering child.

Mostly however their dreams are not so high. Mostly they dream, as most men dream, of long white thighs, and full breasts and the dark place between women's legs. Some dream of it soft and welcoming; some dream of it proud and to be fought for. Some dream pleasure for their beloved and some dream pain for their paid whore, for their defeated enemy, for their chaste neighbour. Some dream women too young with frail fine bodies, long legs like colts and high tight little breasts with icy, frightened nipples; and some dream women too high and noble who would not look at them save with scorn, and dream them humbled and begging.

And to each of them, our song is the promise of the fulfilment of their dream. Just beyond the bowsprit, just beyond the pale light of the moon, there, there, almost within reach, there, waiting to be taken, there, here, now, at once and easily, here, here their dream is waiting and will be given to them.

> Come, sailor; make me a bride gift of your soul
> and I will give you the pearls
> and salt blood of my mouth.

'Come, sailor.' We sing and they come.

The drum beat wavers. The drummer lets his palms go soft, they beat little, desperate, plaintive tattoos that cannot command the muscled backs. The helmsman whimpers; his 'ins' and his 'outs' are no longer orders to be obeyed, but the sobs of each man's longing. The rhythm of the oars breaks down into chaos, and the ship turning a little even in the calm begins to drift towards the shallows.

There is a sudden splash. One has dropped his oar and hurled himself over the gunwhale; we hear his arms beating the water and the heavier breathing as he starts to swim. Now there are shouts from the ship. Not shouts of fear – except for those of course whose fear is the kernel of their lust – but shouts of desire, of longing, of greeting, of joy. There are more splashes, more heavy bodies entering the water, more shouts and anger and laughter and tears.

Most are so perplexed and foolish in their lust that they drown long before they reach our shore. Some are killed by their colleagues as each man fears that the next – who at sunset only a few hours ago was his brother on the rowing bench, his comrade in arms, his dearest friend – may steal the object of his lust, his chosen victim, from him. Those that do not drown, or die at their comrade's hand, come wet and panting to the rocks at our feet and when they have had time to realise the empty hollowness of all they have ever dreamed of, we rend them with our long talons, sear them with our sharp beaks, destroy them with our bright eyes and devour them for our amusement and nourishment.

Then, with the moon high above us, white and harsh on the jagged rocks, we laugh; and for a few moments our pain is softened, our grief is comforted, our anger is slaked, our desire is fulfilled.

This is how it is. This is what we do, because this is what Sirens do and we are Sirens. Sirens, by the deceptive sweetness of their voices, lure brave travellers to their doom.

Down southwards, along the coasts of Sicily, of Demeter's own island, there are many dangers and pitfalls to trap the unwary and unlucky, to snare the bold high-hearted men who bend to the oars and plough the seaway's furrow into the bright future. But of all the perils the peril of the Sirens is the most perilous, not just to life, but to men's souls, because the Sirens break a man on the snares and delusions of his own heart. There is blood and death and malevolence lurking under all desire and the desire for women is the darkest. A woman will take a man from his noble path for her own amusement, for no better motive than spite, for no higher gain than the satisfaction of her own foul lusts and greeds. There is vicious malice always beneath those fair appearances and Sirens are monsters who prove the evil that comes always with female beauty.

They tell the stories of Sirens, so that men may be warned not just when heaving on the rowing bench, or running before a following wind along the rocky, lovely coast of Sicily; but everywhere and always to beware, to beware of sweetness and rest and dreams. To beware of women and of womanly doings.

They tell the end of the story, they do not tell the beginning. They do not tell why we sing and why men must die from our song. They do not tell why we seek for revenge, why we need it and take it and only in taking it can we find any peace.

We will tell you.

She was our duty and our joy. Persephone – our care and our delight. When she had hardly grown into the woman months, into the turnings of the moon, while her cheeks were still smooth and round and her eyes too big for the precious face that carried them, before she was fully grown her mother gave her into our keeping.

Her mother, Demeter, the mother of all living things, Goddess of hill and valley, of flower and fern, of root and bud, tree and leaf, giver of fertility and growth and grace. Just to walk behind Demeter, just to see even the passing of the hem of her skirt as she moved through the fields touching grain stalk and fruit blossom into ripeness, is to have known joy. To look full into her generous face as we did, to help her with her strong labour, to receive as gift the warm smile that makes all plants grow, as we did – we, her chosen nymphs – is to drink deep of the nectar of the earth, to know the music of the world's spiralled dancing, and to live in the richness of springtime.

She gave us her daughter, the most precious of the many things she loved; she gave us her daughter, the beautiful Persephone, daughter of the gods and heir to all loveliness. She gave us Persephone to play with and take care of, while she, Demeter, mother of growth, of seedtime and harvest, was busy about her world-task.

We danced the hills and shores, the bright meadows of Sicily, most pleasing of all the islands, place of vine and olive and corn and wild flowers. We taught the child the music of mountain streams and the song of slow rivers; we taught her the harmony of bird wing and bat flight and the tune the clouds make by day and the stars make by night as they journey across the sky. It is hard to find words for that time, for our joy and our industry. We left nothing undone that we ought to have done and the doing of it was always a pleasure. We loved Persephone, we loved her because we loved her mother and we loved her because she was lovable, loveworthy.

She was innocent and we were careful.

It made no difference.

He came – sudden, dark, fierce. He did not speak. He did not try to woo her or charm her or comfort her. He came in the dark sullen cold of the dead lands where he is King; and she had never known anything but life and warmth. He came with power. With strength. He raped her. It was not enough that he violated her, that he broke her and her dark private blood flowed out on the grass staining it and her. He hurt her. She cried not with authority, but with weakness in a whimpering pain. He raped her and the sun shone unmoved.

We tried to defend her and there was nothing we could do.

Our little white hands beat his back uselessly, so we have grown talons.

Our slim white legs ran to seek help but not swiftly enough, so we have grown wings.

The cold wind of his coming carried our little weak voices into nothingness, so we learned to sing.

His hand smashed against our complaining mouths, blood and saliva on our white little teeth and so now we have beaks of iron.

There is no pain in our drowning sailors that can compare with the pain he inflicted on her.

There is no sadness in men's faces when they see us that can compare with the sadness of Demeter when we told her.

There is no shock in their dying that can compare with the shock when we learned she had consented; had eaten, had taken the six black pomegranate seeds from their sticky luscious red nest. Now that we have watched enough men die we understand better, but then, in our naivety, we thought that to consent, to eat, to live rather than to die, meant that she had chosen. Now we know that sometimes, when there is no choice, when there is nothing that will change how the humiliation is, then it is sometimes necessary to consent because that is the one, the only, thing that you can do; that you must do to be other than victim, to be yourself. That is a real thing and the worst thing.

We searched for her, with her mother, high and low, in heaven and on earth, and Demeter never reproached us. She did not reproach us. Her sadness became madness; became long days of weeping and long nights of wailing. She left the buds to rot on the tree, the grapes to stay unripened on the vine, the standing corn uneared unloved. She howled the dark moors and cursed the birds on the wing, but she did not reproach us.

We asked Zeus himself to return her to us. We humbled ourselves to ask him, as a favour, to give us back what was ours in the first place. And he laughed.

He laughed and told us that he thought it did not matter. He told us that the Dark Lord, his brother, was an honourable mate for Persephone, was a fitting lover for that sweet child. He told us that Hell, the place of shadows, could be a fine home for someone born and brought up in the sunshine. He told her mother not to be so foolish. He said that now she was deflowered there was nothing better she could hope for. And he laughed.

In the end, irritated by Demeter's insistence, rather than moved by her grief, he allowed Persephone to come home for half the year: he made a gift out of what was her right. He felt generous and thought we should be grateful.

We are teaching him gratitude now. Are the sailors who drown grateful? Does the flesh we eat give thanks? Our seductions are sweeter than his was, and we kill our lovers rather than make them drag out long years in the darkness.

Sometimes, at the moon's setting, we wonder, we wonder if our vengeance has hurt us as much as it hurts them. We cannot dance in the sunlit fields any more, we cannot accompany Demeter on her joyful wandering. We cannot comb Persephone's hair or dance with her in the springtime. Instead we must wait here.

We wait; we wait, we sing and we destroy.

This is what Sirens do. We wait for the coming of strong men and by the deceptive sweetness of our voices we lure them to their doom. We are Sirens, this is what we do.

We break a man on the snares and delusions of his own heart. For our own amusement, for no better motive than spite, for no higher gain than the satisfaction of our own foul lusts and greeds.

There is vicious malice always beneath those fair appearances and we are monsters who prove the evil that comes always with female beauty. But our malice is not without cause; our cruelty is small payment for men's lust.

She was defenceless and he raped her. He raped her and went unpunished.

When they die, the sailors, when they drown or kill each other or are eaten while the moon shines high above us, white and harsh on the jagged rocks, we laugh; and for a few moments our pain is softened, our grief is comforted, our anger is slaked, our desire is fulfilled.

It will not last forever, our waiting. The priestess of the oracle has spoken: when a man comes, a single man, who does not respond to our singing, who passes by unmoved, whose desires are pure, without greed, without lust, then our waiting will be over and we will be free again.

We know that one day he will come. Odysseus, the shrewd one, red-headed, limping, pitching his sly good sense against the power of all the songs: the one who looked on Helen and was not moved, the one whose desire is simply to be home with his own woman, so that we have nothing to offer him.

We know he will come. We do not know if we will be glad or sorry. We do not know if we will be able to rest; we do not know if she, her despairing cries, wild against the shock and pain, will let us rest; we do not know if we want to rest.

And until he comes, whenever there is, in the summer months, a fleeting moment of something sweeter than silence – a magical hush; whenever the soft irregular rhythms of the calm sea's rise and fall, rise and fall, rise and fall, rise and fall, become so monotonous, so expected and so gentle, that they fit perfectly to heartbeat and to breathing; whenever out on the sea-way there is a slow roll of water, a gentle heave and a flowing gleam of phosphorescence, and we know a porpoise is passing on its long travels; whenever these nights are upon us, we will be waiting, waiting and singing.

In the name of all the gods, we are justified when we seek vengeance; for our malice is not without cause; our cruelty is small payment for men's lust.

Love Finds Shirley Tempest

FIONA COOPER

MAY WAS in charge of them all, well, she was seven and the rest of them were threes and fours and two-and-a-halfs and fives. She'd been in charge for over a year now. Out in the back lane of Summer Street her word was law and if you didn't obey then you weren't playing and that was that.

They built houses out the back on the bombed site of number thirty-seven. The walls of the houses were a line of broken bricks with a stick for the doors and rags draped for curtains. There was even real carpet, dragged from the bins. You had to wipe your feet before you came in and you couldn't jump over the bricks or you got sent to prison, inside the sooty debris of the old coal bunker. No one wanted to go there, it was damp and stank of rotten green; there were spiders and beetles and slugs.

That summer a new girl came along, Shirley. She was seven, like May, and she came from Swallow Road, two streets up, and all the other bairns there were older. Sick of fetching and carrying or being tied up and rescued, she strayed down to Summer Street and hung around on the edge of the bomb site one morning, watching. There were seven little 'uns and May.

'Eat your breakfasts now,' May told the bairns, all sitting in the kitchen with a heap of dandelions and stones for bread and marmalade. 'And then go out and play while I clear up. John, you go to the shops with Eddy first.'

She put a plate covered with yellow scribbled paper on the pile of bricks she was using as a stove.

'Look,' she said, 'you girls peg out the washing. It's a lovely day for drying.'

Shirley hovered. She wanted in. She raked one hand in the pocket of her dress.

'Knock knock,' she said, standing next to the stick doorway.

'Someone's at the door,' May said. 'Ella, go and see who it is.'

Ella pushed the stick kitchen door and walked down the passage between the lines of brick. She pulled the stick front door open and looked up at Shirley.

'Yes?' she said.

'Hello,' Shirley said, 'I'm Shirley, I've come to see your mam. Is she in?'

'She might be busy,' Ella said. 'Wait on.'

She ran back to the kitchen.

'May – mam, it's a lady to see you.'

'Who is it?' May said.

'It's – I dunno.'

'Didn't you ask her?' May said, dusting her hands against her skirt and bustling to the front door.

'You know what bairns are like,' she said to Shirley, 'can I help you?'

'I've come for a cup of tea,' Shirley said, holding out some sweets, 'I brought some biscuits. I'm Shirley.'

'I'm Mrs Summer,' May said, 'but you can call me May.'

'I'm Mrs Swallow of course, but you can call me Shirley,' Shirley said. 'Bairns are such a worry, aren't they?'

'It's terrible,' May said, just like her own mam, 'you'll have to take us as you find us. Come in.'

Shirley followed her in, remembering to close the door behind her.

'Now then,' May said, 'my friend Mrs Swallow has come round for a chat and we can't be doing with you under our feet. Get yourselves outside and enjoy the fresh air while it's sunny.'

'It's not sunny,' Eddy said, 'May, it's not sunny.'

'Mam,' May said, 'and what's that?'

She pointed to the yellow covered plate. John nudged Eddy.

'That means the sun's out, Eddy,' he said, 'don't get cross with him, mam, he's only four.'

'He's old enough to think,' May said, 'and if he did, I might have a minute to think myself. Now, Eddy, are you getting out in the sunshine or do I have to tell your father?'

'Come on,' John said, Eddy was his brother after all, 'let's go to the shop in the sunshine.'

He dragged Eddy out of the kitchen and May put her hands on her hips.

'I've more grey hairs than—' she said. 'If it's not one thing it's another. And what with piecework and The Drink, he never turns up his money and I don't know how I fill seven mouths seven days a week, I really don't.'

'I don't have any bairns,' Shirley said, 'what with the shop and mother in bed, I've never had the time. I don't mind though, I'm always full of busy.'

'No bairns?' May said, staring at her. She couldn't imagine a house without bairns. 'I'll put the kettle on.'

Ella wanted a drink. A proper drink, May, sorry, mam, not just pretendy. Eddy and John were hungry for real bread and jam. Marie needed a wee. And so did Irene. And Thomas had messed his nappy. Only little Billy was quiet, and he was asleep in his great big Silver Cross pram.

'Honestly,' May said, 'I'll be glad when this day's over. If it's not one thing it's another. Marie take Irene to the netty. John, take your Thomas in for his nappy and get some bread and jam off your mam. Eddy, you need to get coal in for the fire.'

Eddy stared at her and started wailing.

'Coal, man,' John said. 'You daft little sod, *that's* the coal heap, and *there's* the fire.'

He pointed to the gravel heap and a cardboard box in the living room.

'Do I put the stones there?' Eddy said, licking tears away. 'Do I John? Is that what I do, May?'

'Our Eddy's a bit—' May whispered loudly. Then all singsong, 'That's a good lad, Eddy, get the coal. It looks like stones but we're playing, Eddy. And the box is a fire. JOHN! Get him his teddy, he'll never settle.'

She leaned towards Shirley.

'He's happy if he's trailing his teddy round with him,' she said. 'He should be past it at four, but he's always been a bit—'

Shirley watched Eddy scoop up stones and wander towards the box.

'You've just been through the walls,' Ella said, 'May, Eddy's just been through the walls, can I be the policeman and put him in prison, can I, May?'

'He's only a bairn,' May yelled at her, 'you should be helping him, not picking on him!'

'Our house is always like this,' she said grandly to Shirley. 'Whatever will you think of us, Mrs Swallow?'

'I think you're a marvel, Mrs Summer,' Shirley said, 'a marvel!'

'Oh,' May said, blushing, 'that kettle will be boiled dry by now!'

John came back with jam and bread and Thomas. Irene

and Marie came back hand in hand giggling, they always giggled when they'd had a wee and compared belly buttons and knickers. Ella found a broken bit of wood for a shovel for Eddy and was showing him what to do.

'Well, here's your supper,' May said, taking the jam and bread, 'come on now, there's not enough hot for baths tonight. It'll have to be a lick and a promise.'

She took the yellow plate down and wrapped it in creased tin foil, burnt golden and black from cooking.

'See, it's night time,' she said, putting the shiny plate on the pile of bricks. 'The moon's up already and it's past your bedtime.'

'Do I sit here, May, do I?' Eddy said anxiously, 'Mam, I mean.'

'You're a good boy doing all that coal for your mam,' May said. 'Yes, you sit here and have your jam and bread. Then you bairns get to sleep and be quiet and I'll have a minute's peace to talk to Mrs Swallow, my friend.'

'I'll tell them a story,' Shirley said. 'It helps good dreams to come.'

She sat by them on the ground and told them a mixture of The Gingerbread Man and Snow White, then shushed them and tiptoed away.

She and May sat by the box full of stones and sipped invisible tea. The other children were lying down all over the bomb site and kept their eyes closed.

'Ee,' May said, 'it's good to get the weight off. Perhaps you're right not having bairns, Mrs Swallow. God love them, but they do wear you out.'

'Can we get up yet?'

'Is it morning?'

May said, 'Shh!' and pointed to the silvery plate.

'It's the only time I get,' she said to Shirley. 'It's the best time, time for a bit of peace with the moon shining up above us all.'

'Look at the stars!' Shirley said. 'There's a shooting star, May, make a wish!'

'I wish,' May said, then giggled. 'You daft bugger, you talk like it's real.'

'It is,' Shirley said, 'it's magic.'

That was their first summer together and they played every day. Shirley's aunt was glad she had a friend and they went to the park with all the bairns and they sat on the swings and dreamed. They went to the same school and walked along the road arm in arm and told each other everything. You didn't see May without Shirley and you didn't see Shirley without May. One day they nicked cuts in their palms and swore they'd be best friends forever, watching the blood ooze into bright red beads.

May went to the factory when she was sixteen, and Shirley stayed at school. Her aunt, Catherine Tempest, ran the pop shop on Swallow Road and she fiercely wanted Shirley to do well. May's mam, Nadine Westerhope, needed May's wage and May liked dancing and boys and got embarrassed by seeing her best friend still in a school uniform when she came through the factory gates full of chat and laughter. But on a weekend they were close like they'd always been.

'Our Shirley,' Catherine said in the shop, picking over a pile of clothes, 'college now, doesn't the time fly? No sign of a young man, yet, but she's happy with her daft films and books. I hope she's happy. She never tells me much, like.'

'Aye,' Nadine said, 'our May's got herself—, you know. So there's wedding bells. He's not a bad lad, Stan, but I could have wished . . . Never mind, I've always had a house full of bairns and another'll make no—'

'Difference,' Catherine added automatically. 'Shirley was asking after her when she was home last. I'm sure she'd like to go to the wedding.'

'Oh it'll be register office,' Nadine said. 'Money's tight, Cath, but when is it not? Mind, there'll be a do at The Blue Horizon after. I'll let you know.'

And she did, but Catherine forgot to tell Shirley until it was too late. Shirley sent flowers and a card and May kept the card in the family Bible.

Shirley made a film for Channel Four when she was twenty-eight. She didn't tell her aunt, since it was about two women in love, and what would the neighbours say? It was shown at half past midnight, when May was waiting for Stan to come home. He didn't like her to go to bed first, and the last time she had, he'd knocked seven colours of shit out of her. If it was just her, she'd be off, but there was little Graham and Shirley and Nadine to think of. Shirley was five and Graham was six and Nadine was one and a half and she had an awful feeling that soon there'd be another. Stan could knock her silly and still want to *do it*, in fact all the more; the bastard seemed to get turned on after he'd got her crying and begging him to stop. And everyone knew, they must, the walls were thin and everyone knew everything, but no one said anything to her face.

She yawned on the sofa, flicking channels.

She saw the name Shirley Tempest and frowned.

Shirley Tempest?

Couldn't be.

Then she watched the film. It was beautiful: all trees and waterfalls and two women who started off friends and suddenly they were kissing under the moonlight. Iris and Daisy, wild and pretty as flowers. It gave her a warm ache deep inside; it was so gentle. The women looked at each other and smiled and slowly took each other's clothes off, and May was scandalised and thrilled. Bugger it, she made a cup of tea to keep awake, and when Stan came in full of beer and hell, she just let it all wash over her and when he rolled on top of her she closed her eyes and thought of Shirley's film. And when he'd done his business and lay snoring, she went to the window and looked at the moon and cried and cried, missing Shirley and wondering where the magic had gone and how it had all got this way.

She thought of writing to her, but it seemed daft, what could she say? Here I am, Shirley, just like we swore we'd never be, a houseful of bairns and a man I cannot stand the sight of, and there you are, getting famous. Is it lasses with you, Shirley, you're a sly bugger. Do you remember . . . ?

But Shirley wouldn't want to hear from her. And she wouldn't know where to send it, anyway.

Shirley sat in Cannes, watching her film for the zillionth time. It had won an award and she wanted someone to celebrate with. She had a contract for a series now, enough money to relax with and an ache in her heart. For she could film true love; she could film romance so that people cried and looked at her with wonder, but she'd never found anyone to look at her the way her heroines looked at each other; no one to walk with by waterfalls; no one to get naked with and laugh. They said she made dreams come true and that hers was a magic eye and she smiled distantly and thanked them.

They were OK, these people, but none of them knew her. If she talked about her childhood she could see images of sepia tinted nostalgia form in their eyes. Sepia tinted or gritty monochrome, like the first episodes of Coronation Street. No use to tell them how in the summer all the girls wore skirts or dresses like gaudy summer flowers, and how May clacked along the back lanes in discarded pink stilettos, coal dust for eye-shadow and pilfered lipstick. Or how she borrowed scarves and blouses from her auntie's shop and dressed up like Scarlett O'Hara. She didn't talk about any of it these days.

What could she say?

I went back last year to see my auntie. I went to where May lives, seventeen Woodbine Close, but I didn't

*knock. You see, there was shouting and banging inside,
and the neighbours over the road were all busy with
their front yards so they could listen. I didn't want to
know what had happened. I took champagne, you see,
but I brought it home with me again. Auntie Cath said,
'Divent waste it, pet, save it for summat special.' And I
felt like I was visiting where she lives, May, and I don't
belong there any more and I miss her.*

She wondered if May remembered how they'd practised
kissing when they were fourteen, shocked and thrilled by each
other's tongues, making bleeagh! faces and laughing themselves stupid.

Iris and Daisy dissolved into soft focus pink and she
smiled, acknowledging the applause.

Five years later on Swallow Road, the sun wasn't out, but
Shirley wore sunglasses anyway, it stopped people getting
through to her eyes.

'That friend of yours, May – ee, what a carry on! That Stan
she was married to, well, he took a knife to her and the police
was called and all sorts. He's left the area and good riddance, I
say, She's had a hell of a life wi' him!'

'I thought I might go and see her.'

'Get yersel' away, pet. May could use some company!'

She knocked at seventeen Woodbine Close.

A little girl answered the door.

'Is your mam in?' Shirley said, 'I'm Shirley.'

'She's in the kitchen,' said the little girl, 'she might be busy.
I dunno. Mam! It's a lady to see you!'

'Well who is it, man?'

'It's Shirley,' she called.

'Never in God's!' May came into the passage.

She hadn't changed. Good god, fifteen years since she'd
seen her and she hadn't changed. Sure, her waist was thicker,

103

there were lines of worry on her brow and lines of tears and laughter round her eyes. Her mane of hair was short with a few strands of silver among the glossy black curls. But her eyes were the same.

'Ee,' May said, 'I don't know. You'll have to take us as you find us. Bairns under my feet, you pick your moments. Howay, Shirley, come through, I'll put the kettle on.'

She picked up toys and magazines as they went through, fussing and faffing until Shirley said, 'May, man, it's you I've come to see,' and that broke the awkwardness. They drank tea and the children gawped at Shirley's gold bracelets and rings. She was in films. She was a film star. And she was their mam's friend sitting just like anyone else in their kitchen.

'Look at the clock,' May said at half past eight. 'Get yourselves to bed. Lick and a promise. I don't know where the time's got to.'

'I'll come and tell you a story when you're in bed,' Shirley said. 'If there's a fridge in the house, May, dig in my bag.'

May sat in the sudden quiet of the empty kitchen, feet thundering upstairs, Shirley laughing and talking nineteen to the dozen, just like years ago. Dig in my bag! Well, that was Shirley, her bag was leather soft as silk, a clutter of papers and keys and jewellery and expensive perfume. And a bottle of champagne. Champagne and Shirley in Woodbine Close! And her with nothing suitable to drink from. She lit a candle and the chaos of the room disappeared in shadow.

'They promise to go to sleep,' Shirley said, 'God, they're lovely, May. Hard work, eh?'

'This is the only time I get,' May said. 'And you and your posh champagne. I've only got cups.'

Shirley laughed.

'Used to be jam jars, remember?' she said.

'Where did the years go?' May said. 'Well, you've been busy making films. Your Auntie Cath's as proud as—'

'And you've not been idle,' Shirley said, 'I couldn't cope with bairns. Never. Not like you. I like to borrow them and hand them back. I'm a hell of a good auntie.'

'I didn't have a lot of choice,' May said. 'And it's been better since I hoyed His Highness out. Graham had his wild times, but he's happy now. Christ, Shirley, man, there's been hell on here.'

'I should have come and rescued you,' Shirley said. 'Cheers!'

'I've seen your film,' May said. 'That one about Iris and Daisy. Years ago. Then I saw you on that late night arty farty show. You've gone geet lah-di-dah, only it's still you. I almost wrote to you. Your films, are they all ... you know?'

'About women?' Shirley said. 'Yes. I wish you had written.'

'Ah,' May said, 'I didn't know what to say. But I think you could be right. Fellas is awful, well, mine was. What's she like?'

'Who?'

'Your girlfriend, man!'

'I don't have one,' Shirley said. 'No one seems – right.'

A frisson went through May, like when they'd pretend kissed each other, like when she'd seen that film. She looked at her old friend and it was strange. There was the expensive haircut and the clothes and the voice, but her eyes were just the same, now she'd taken those dark glasses off. Maybe more troubled, sadder even, but that could just be the shadows from the candle and the fire. Older and sadder, that was life. Wasn't it? It never occurred to her that Shirley's skin was alive with the same frisson.

A glass of champagne later, Shirley spoke.

'You always had such lovely hair,' she said. 'My auntie called me Shirley, you know, I think she wanted blonde curls like Shirley Temple. Only mine was straight as a board mousey. I always loved your curls.'

She reached out and touched May's hair. May stayed still,

but her heart was pounding as she crept upstairs to check the bairns.

'I'm just nipping back to Auntie Cath's,' Shirley said, 'there's something I almost forgot.'

'Leave the latch,' May said. 'You can let yourself back in.'

Alone again, she brushed her hair hard so it crackled. She ran her finger over her teeth and scrubbed her knuckles into her cheeks. She felt fourteen years old again; fourteen when they spent every waking minute together, slept at each other's houses and life was an adventure to dream about.

'I'm back,' Shirley said. 'Here's another bottle.'

'I shall get tipsy,' May said. 'But who cares?'

'Oh, I care,' Shirley said.

May sucked the bubbles against her teeth until they stung.

They talked and laughed and May found the radio station that plays old records from ten at night till three in the morning. She went to the toilet, feeling giddy and happy and sat scolding her imagination. Just enjoy the evening, May, you daft cow, she thought. And don't keep her here too long, she'll not want to waste hours yapping with you, just because you're lonely.

Later, she spoke into one of Shirley's stories.

'Just look at the time – oh!'

Instead of the clock, there was a shining disc, a plate wrapped in tinfoil.

'You daft bugger,' May said, 'fancy you remembering that! Where did it come from?'

'Auntie Cath's kitchen,' Shirley said, 'she thinks I've gone crackers. The best time of the day, you always said. Time for bed. A bit of peace.'

The radio played *I'll stop just behind the moon and wait for you*, and May stared at the fire until she could hardly see it. Then she heard Shirley's voice, soft and shy.

'Time for me and you? May, can you hear me?'

'Are you sure?' May said. 'You don't have to.'

'Are *you* sure?' Shirley said. 'I've been sure ever since I saw you in the hallway tonight. I've been sure ever since I came down to Summer Street when I was seven years old. Only I didn't know what I was sure of.'

'Come here then,' May said. 'Let's do some more of that kissing – only I'm not practising this time. I want real kisses.'

'You always were bossy,' Shirley said, holding her close.

'You always needed organising.'

'I always needed you.'

'Are we right in the head?' May said. 'What about the bairns?'

'We'll get a nanny,' Shirley said. 'How long do you need to pack?'

'There's only one thing I'm taking with me,' May said. 'And you brought that into this house tonight.'

Years later, she swore it was the champagne talking, and Shirley said thank God for the night they invented champagne. They had a house in the hills near Los Angeles and three children who talked with a Geordie/American twang. The youngest babbled pure Hollywood. When people came to see them they admired the paintings and the sculpture and the beautiful rugs. Shirley would tell stories about where they'd bought them and when. And after dinner, they'd sit down by the log fire and their eyes were drawn to a shiny silver disc on the wall and they'd gaze at it and wonder and ask.

But neither May nor Shirley would say anything about it, just look at each other like there was no one else in the room. Unless they were pressed, and then one of them would smile and nod at the other to speak.

'That's magic,' they'd say. 'Just magic.'

And the silvery plate gleamed golden in the firelight, glowing like a harvest moon.

Chalk Mother

LIZA CODY

ON THE morning of my daughter's wedding day I woke up with a hangover. There were hot needles in my eyes. I sprawled like a washed-up starfish on the daybed in the studio, squinting furiously at the good north light. Day was an unwelcome visitor knocking at the window with the worst of bad news.

'Go away,' I said. But it didn't.

The night before a wedding is reserved, by rights, for the bridegroom to behave badly, not the bride's mother. But the bridegroom was too sensible. There was no rude, crude stag party, no dying gasp for the bachelor.

My daughter phoned me at seven in the evening and said, 'Everything's ready, Mum. Davey and I made the vol-au-vent cases. All we have to do in the morning is fill them.'

'Vol-au-vents,' I said, wincing. I had picked up the receiver without first putting down my paint brush and of course I jabbed my eyebrow with finest hog's hair bristles loaded with French ultramarine.

'I told you,' my daughter said, kind and patient. 'Vol-au-vents. Seven different canapes. Davey's mother will bring the smoked salmon in the morning.'

'What's Davey up to?' I said.

'He's icing the chocolate gateau,' she said. 'He doesn't like wedding cake so we made a sort of multi-layered *sacher torte*. Davey's mother thinks we're crazy.' She giggled gently at their craziness.

'No stag party then?' I said to deflect her from the madness of chocolate icing.

'Don't be silly, Mum,' my daughter said.

My daughter. Conceived somewhere on the road to Marrakesh, by someone enchanting whose name I never knew. My daughter who danced in my belly to Bedouin music. Who sat on my shoulders at the Stones concert in the park. Who slept in my lap at the Round House while the Red Buddha Theatre performed. Who sulked in the rain at Greenham Common.

Once, we were so broke I shoplifted tins of baked beans from Tesco's to feed her. I made her a cloak of many colours from my own clothes when she grew out of her winter coat. She loved her cloak and swanned around in it like a fairy-tale princess. I made her a mobile of the sun, the moon and all the planets. But she wanted a Barbie doll. I couldn't afford a Barbie, so she cried.

At about that time I made peace with my own mother and *she* gave my daughter a Barbie doll. She also gave her a good winter wool coat to go to school in. My daughter put away her cloak of many colours and afterwards only brought it out to play dressing-up with her friends.

When she was eleven I took her to the opening of my first exhibition in New York. There was snow on the ground. The air sparkled and cab door-handles tingled with dry electricity. She adored the Radio City Christmas pageant but she spent the whole week worried about missing school.

The next time I went to New York my daughter chose to stay at home with my mother.

'She needs stability,' my mother said. 'She's at that insecure age.' I couldn't deny it.

'Do you really *have* to go?' my daughter said.

'Stay,' my mother said. 'Your agent can handle the exhibition.' At the time my mother was teaching my daughter to clean filigree silver with a baby's toothbrush. I looked into two pairs of beautiful cobalt blue eyes.

'Stay,' they said. But I went. When I came back, my mother's silver sparkled like fresh New York snow and my daughter had been given a dove-grey suit, silk and wool mix, with matching gloves. She left the suit for safekeeping at my mother's house. She was afraid I might, in a fit of absent-mindedness, mistake it for a paint rag.

My lover brought me Sancerre and white peaches for my fortieth birthday. My daughter introduced him to her friends as her stepfather. My lover left in a huff.

The first time my daughter came home with a boyfriend herself they sat in the kitchen drinking hot chocolate until two in the morning. I was working so I didn't know they were there. She told me about it the next day.

'He stayed until *two*, but nothing happened,' she said proudly.

'Why didn't you bring him into the studio?' I asked.

'You were working,' she said. She lowered long silky lashes to hide the cobalt blue eyes. 'I showed him your catalogues, though. He was very impressed. He's never met a proper artist before. His father works for British Airways.'

My daughter has eyelashes like the highest quality sable brushes, like a fringe of soft fern around a deep blue pond. I cannot paint her eyes. I tried several times but I always failed.

'Don't be silly, Mum,' my daughter says at seven in the evening, eighteen hours before her wedding. 'Davey doesn't want a stag party. He wants to keep a clear head for tomorrow. Besides there's so much to do.'

'Well,' I said, 'if Davey won't have a stag party, I shall have to throw a hag party.'

'Oh *Mum*!' my daughter said. And she laughed. She has a throaty, gentle laugh. 'Don't forget you have to go to the hairdresser in the morning.'

'Oh God,' I said.

'And Grandma's picking you up at eleven so you must be ready.'

'That's too much,' I protested. 'I'm quite capable of driving myself.'

'Of course you are,' she said. 'If you remember.'

I have never forgotten anything of importance to my daughter. I was there, *on time*, for parent–teacher meetings, school plays, dentists, doctors, trains, birthday parties. Only once did I screw up, and that was the time I was supposed to meet her plane when she was returning from a holiday in Nice. I arrived at Heathrow at the right time but a day late. She was perfectly okay – she had taken a taxi to my mother's. One measly day late and I was branded forever as a numbskull where appointments are concerned.

'You know what you're like,' my daughter said. She has the kind of smile you can hear on the phone.

She has taken great comfort over the years from the notion that I am eccentric, artistic and incapable of rational behaviour. She is normal – I am weird. She is steady – I am erratic. She is practical – I am... No, not romantic. *She* is romantic, and if she is romantic I must be, of necessity, something else. She has defined herself, and in doing so she has defined me as her opposite. Black and white. Chalk and cheese. We are inextricably coupled but utterly different.

Oddly enough, I am grateful for her definitions – they have allowed her to forgive me for not being the mother she wanted. How could I be when we are chalk and cheese? How can cheese be a proper mother to chalk?

Chalk mothers buy clothes at Marks and Spencer, not Oxfam. Chalk mothers have husbands, not lovers. Chalk mothers do *not* roll joints. My daughter should have had a chalk mother like *my* mother. I'm glad there was one in the family. Unfortunately for my daughter, she was mine and not hers.

'Mum,' she says to me, over the telephone, the night before her wedding. 'I know marriage is against your religion, but it won't seem so bad if you could think of it as a rite of passage.'

She thinks, you see, that I didn't marry because I don't believe in marriage. She thinks I chose not to marry, that I chose my work instead. It suits her to believe that I was strong enough to make such a choice, and that it was important enough to deprive her of a father. Nothing less than a matter of belief and principle would do. A sweet night under a tropic moon is not good enough. The momentary love of a stranger can't be love – it is feckless. Love is forever, says my daughter.

But nothing is forever. Yesterday I had to admit, finally, that I could not carry on working at night without spectacles. Even standing, with a drawing at arm's length, I could not force my eyes to focus. A line which should have been hard-edged, nervous and black as a spider's leg was furry, soft and grey as a spider's web. I stood for half an hour, trying to sweat it out. I could focus clearly on the line by standing so far back that I couldn't stretch to touch the paper. I could see, and I could draw. But not at the same time.

I went out immediately to the late-night chemist and bought a pair of half-glasses but I couldn't bring myself to wear them. I sat in the studio, doing nothing, grieving for my eyesight. Now *that* is what I call a rite of passage.

'Old,' I said. 'Eye and I are getting old.'

'What?' my daughter says. 'You're mumbling. Have you been smoking? Don't smoke, Mum, it isn't good for you, and I don't want Davey to think his mother-in-law is just an old hippy.'

That hurt. 'Old hippy' I could just about take. But 'Davey's mother-in-law'? That hit hard. Davey's mother-in-law wasn't me. Davey's mother-in-law was a stranger with a stern face and cheap reading glasses bought on the spur of the moment from a late-night chemist.

And Davey himself was too sensible for a stag night. Davey was spending the night before his wedding putting the finishing touches to a sort of layered *sacher torte*. His last wild fling – a brown cake instead of a white one. Ah, the young are so adventurous.

So I threw a hag party for him: a little wine, a little dope, some Greek bread, black olives and a few old friends. I was not too sensible for a last spasm of freedom before becoming 'Davey's mother-in-law'. We played loud music and danced in the studio while my daughter slept snug in her safe white bed, and the vol-au-vent cases rested in the fridge.

'This is a hag party,' I told my friends. 'This is my last wild fling before turning, willy-nilly, into a mother-in-law.'

Friends raised rosy red glasses in the candlelight and drank to my daughter. They all knew her – my *doppelgänger* – from the old days. I drank to her too – over and over again – dancing to 'Wild Horses' and 'Moonlight Mile'. Old rockers never die – they merely lose their eyesight and, grudgingly, become mothers-in-law.

On the morning of my daughter's wedding day I breakfasted on black coffee and white aspirin. And, because I try not to rebel against my daughter the way I rebelled against my mother, I went to the hairdresser to be scissored, pinned and polished.

'Please,' my daughter said, the night before. 'Have a proper haircut – just this once. No hacking with nail scissors in front of the bathroom mirror.'

Tamed, I went home and dressed in the clothes my daughter had chosen for me.

'I had to choose,' she told me. Kind and patient. 'You'd

have put it off and put it off until there was no time left. You'd have come to my wedding in denim.'

She chose silk the colour of newborn moss, and I wasn't offended. I like silk, and I like moss. My daughter would be wearing silk too: silk the colour of buttermilk.

But when I looked in the mirror I saw a figure of quiet, subtle restraint. I saw Davey's mother-in-law. I saw someone who would wear spectacles, who would be surprised by chocolate wedding cake.

I simply couldn't help it – I found a long silk scarf to wind around my throat. Even after so many years it glowed like dying embers which only need a breath to revive them. Ashes of roses, embroidered with a little lapis lazuli, pale turquoise and a touch of crimson. The scarf did not cure my hangover. But I could see perfectly. I could see two kids, younger than my daughter and sensible Davey are today. I saw them lying together under a huge tropic moon. I saw their kiss.

In the morning he gave me a silk scarf, and went on his way. It was a wedding without benefit of church or chocolate cake. Feckless, my daughter would say, with her kindly, patient smile. But I never regretted it – even though my daughter is chalk and her mother is cheese.

Trouser Ladies

SHENA MACKAY

ONE BY one the pumpkins, heavy orange lamps glowing against the deepening blue dusk, are carried into the shop and extinguished. Oranges, lemons, satsumas, pomegranates follow in procession, and when the greengrocer's grass, bleached by street lights now, is rolled up in a strip of muddy turf, the woman watching from her window turns away into her own life in a room lit by tangerine glass globes and fans. A low band of sound runs past her like a pattern etched into the glass, a dado on the wallpaper, so familiar that she hasn't heard it for years, and besides, Beatrice at seventy-six is becoming a little deaf. Her white hair is still thick, while the embroidered kimono she is wearing, for she is in the process of getting ready to go out, has faded from peacock to azure and worn to patches of gossamer grids and loose hammocks of threads slung between blossoms and birds. She has let herself be diverted by the street because she is apprehensive about the evening, fearing that it will be an uneasy walk down a Memory Lane signposted by someone else's reminiscences, made strange like a road in a dream. She is a journalist who has been photographed in battledress and

117

safari suit in theatres of war and cinema foyers, who is in a blue funk at the thought of meeting the daughter of her best and dearest, now dead, friend in the neutral territory of a restaurant. Catriona Ling had seen the announcement of Beatrice Alloway's birthday in the paper, had telephoned her, and was probably regretting her impulse as much as Beatrice rued her surprised acceptance.

Chinese lanterns and bronze and yellow chrysanthemums, birthday tokens, are crammed into a bizarre jug on a low table and a glass rectangle in front of the tiny black grate-basket; and on the mantelpiece, at the centre of a jumble of cards and invitations, is a branch of spindle berries in a blue conical pottery vase. Beatrice bought them herself, making her birthday the excuse for extravagance. They cost her six pounds, but she had to have them. She catches her breath each time she sees the matt, deep pinkish-red four-lobed fruits opening in the warmth of the room to a flight of wingcases across the cobalt-blue wall, flaunting their orange seeds. One of Bee's birthday cards, the one from Catriona's twin sisters, had cast a blight of unease over her birthday. Although it is hidden by another card, it obtrudes as she gazes at the spray of spindle, and remembers Betty's excitement when they came upon a spindle tree, the first any of them had seen, at the edge of a little wood in Kent more than forty years ago.

It had been the Sunday afternoon of Beatrice's ill-conceived visit to Canterbury. What she had hoped or imagined would come from a descent on Betty's domesticity she did not know then and couldn't say now, just that she had been overcome by longing to see her again. Beatrice Alloway and Betty Gemmell had grown up together in Ardrossan, gone to school and university together, and then Betty had married Alec Ling, the boy next door. Betty and Alec, and their son, wee Donald, went to London to seek their fortune, found that the streets were not paved with gold, and now Alec was a miner, digging away in the Kent coalfield, wondering what to do next to support a growing family. Beatrice's unannounced arrival had caused a confusion that had sent them all – Alec, Betty, Donald, the twins Heather and Erica and four-year-old Catriona – out on this awkward walk, looking forward to teatime scones and a lopsided sponge cake. Suddenly there was the spindle tree, exotic and English, with red leaves and pink fruit trembling on delicate stalks in the blue autumn sky. Heather and Erica held up the baby dolls Beatrice had brought, to admire the berries, and Beatrice wished that the whole lot of them, Alec and the children, would prick their fingers on a spindle and fall asleep, like the Sleeping Beauty's court, so that she and Betty could be alone together.

Then, like the good sport she was, Auntie Bee was instigating a game of hide-and-seek, whooping through falling leaves, bobbing up behind bushes and letting the children pelt her with damp handfuls of red and brown and yellow, chasing them round tree trunks.

The smell of kicked-up leaves, fungus and lichen is pungent in her head as she opens her wardrobe and takes out the black suit in which she will face the evening. The trouble was, and is, Betty Gemmell was the love of her life, and she was Betty's best friend.

Ting-a-ling-ling goes the old-fashioned black bell on the shop door, saying our names because it belongs to us, the Ling twins, Heather and Erica, Erica and Heather – our names were father's little joke. He loved all ericacaea, and sprinkled sand on our cloddy garden to make them feel at home. When we moved into our brand-new council house in Canterbury, all the gardens were raw, shining clay; like everybody else, we planted vegetables and chrysanthemums and Esther Reeds, big white daisies or marguerites that the children took to harvest festival, in firm solid bunches with a blob of carnations at the centre like the jam on semolina, but only father grew heathers and dwarf conifers in crazy paving. Mother only liked heather when it was growing wild, in Scotland, where our family came from. She hated dwarf conifers. We had moved down South in 1948, first to dismal lodgings where we were all very unhappy, and then to our new house, east of the Martyr's Memorial, near a railway bridge where you could stand and let the trains puff great cornets of pink and white steam and smoke over you so that it was like being at the heart of an ice-cream. Canterbury had been badly bombed in the War, and when you were out playing you came on half-houses rising from the rubble of buddleia, willowherb and toadflax, smashed bricks and glass and porcelain, and rolls of brambles and barbed wire. You squeezed through the corrugated iron that fenced off the wasteland and found heaps of jagged slates for tomahawks lying among the nettles. Once a gang of us discovered a shining pile of aluminium off-cuts that made swords and arrows beyond our wildest dreams. A boy called Goldfish was shot in the tongue, but lived to tell the tale. Of course, it's all changed a lot now, but we can still see it as it was: the streets of little houses behind privet hedges and hydrangeas, with beds visible in front rooms, and old men with two sticks sitting on walls, and people limping along on one big black surgical boot, with a steel stirrup to make their legs the same length. Even now one of us just has to say 'remember' and the smell of our house comes back in whiffs of pastel distemper, bright patterned carpet, the new wood and varnish of the furniture smelling like Lefevres where we bought it, and the ploughed earth of the garden glittering with bits of bottle glass, fragments of pottery and oyster shells.

We can remember school too, vividly, and it's quite strange when one of our old schoolmates comes into the shop accompanied by children or grandchildren, but mostly we get tourists. Our little shop is near the Cathedral and we sell pretty things: angels and illustrated Bibles, silver Canterbury crosses and Celtic jewellery, cards, bookmarks, gargoyles and so forth, and we live in the flat above, overlooking the River Stour and the Westgate towers and gardens. It seems to us that people don't really change, they just grow bigger, and when some middle-aged voice asks for this or that, they might as well be saying, 'Got any fag cards, twin?'

We had. Fat bundles of them, in rubber bands.

'Got any film stars? Who's your favourite film star, twin?'

'Doris Day,' we said. We hadn't seen any of her films but you had to have a favourite film star. Other children queued up after the register for National Savings Stamps with pictures of Prince Charles and Princess Anne, and had scrapbooks of the Royal Family. Our brother Donald belonged to a stamp club, Catriona collected bits of coloured glass which she called her jewels, and woolly caterpillars whom she called her friends; and we latched on to Doris Day. One day our pretend love for her became real. Mother's best friend Beatrice, whom we called Auntie Bee, although we hadn't met her and we only knew her from the Christmas presents she sent us, was a journalist and sometimes she sent Mother magazines and we would fall on them with our blunt scissors in the hopes of finding a picture of Doris Day inside. Pink and white, gingham and golden, laughing eyes as blue as speedwells or periwinkles, with her wide, eager cream-cheese smile, Doris Day was our goddess. Not our ideal, for we knew that we with our ginger hair and scratched legs and floppy cotton socks hadn't a hope of growing into anything resembling Doris. Film stars were an entirely different species then, a race apart; we couldn't tell one from another of this current lot if we wanted to – no grace, no style, no charm, no charisma, no quality, and we're still waiting for the real-life film stars to come back, to descend from Valhalla and reclaim Hollywood.

It must have been about 1951, the year of the Festival of Britain, when we finally got to meet Auntie Bee. At that time, women wearing trousers were a comparatively rare sight, apart from bus conductresses and the occasional brown landgirl in a brown landscape, glimpsed through a bus

121

window. Catriona used to call them 'trouser ladies'. It was a dull autumn Sunday afternoon, wasn't it, and we were sitting reading on the windowsill of our front room, Heather sitting on the left as usual, Erica on the right-hand side and Catriona was standing in the middle, on the little sea-grass stool when suddenly she said, 'Here comes a trouser lady. And she's coming to our house!'

It was true. A trouser lady was coming up our path. She was in our porch. Knocking at our door.

'Beatrice! What a wonderful surprise! I can't believe it's really you!' Mother was laughing and almost crying, hugging the trouser lady. 'Children, this is your Auntie Bee, at long last!'

'Let me look at you all!' said Auntie Bee. 'Donald, Heather, Erica, Catriona! They've all got your red hair Betty! Alec, hello!'

'Just the one bag, Beatrice?' said Father. 'I do hope that this doesn't mean you're not planning a good long stay with us?'

A cold shiver ran through us, Father was smiling, but only the family could tell when he was only pretending to be nice, and sometimes we got it wrong.

'Come away in, pet,' he said. Something had made him cross; perhaps it was that Bee had said we all had Mother's hair.

'Dad's got red hair too,' said Donald. His own was dark red like Father's; Mother's, ours and Catriona's was fiery and crinkly and leapt and sparked at the hairbrush's strokes. We were always losing our ribbons and kirby-grips. Bee had brought us all presents: Meccano for Donald, a teddy bear for Catriona, and twin dolls for us. They were delicate featured, with rosebud mouths and blue eyes that opened and closed, and feathery, painted light-brown hair. One of them had a soft green knitted dress and bonnet tied with ribbons, the other was dressed in lavender blue. We called them Suzannah and Maria. They were very pale, and when we took them to the baby clinic

– Jamie was born about nine months after Bee's visit – the nurse weighed Suzannah and Maria and told us to give them more porridge. We did.

Auntie Bee stayed for five days, and we would race home from school at dinner time and in the afternoon to see her, and she would let us all get into her bed when we took her a cup of tea in the morning. The only thing that spoiled it was Father. He was in a bad mood all the time and argued continuously with Bee. If she had said coal was black, he would have sworn it was white. One teatime he threw his food at the wall and he hit Donald round the head for spilling his milk. The trouble was, Bee didn't know that you had to agree with everything Father said.

Bee tried to put things right. 'Let's all go to the pictures,' she said. At that, Father stormed out to the lodge – which was what everybody called the big sheds in the back gardens – and Mother couldn't come because Catriona was too little. So Bee and Donald and we two set out. It was thrilling; we had never been to the cinema at night, and we twins held tight to Bee's hands. It was like entering a palace, and the curtains across the screen, rippling with magical, ever-changing colours, were the most beautiful things we had ever seen. To make our happiness complete – or it would have been if we hadn't been worried about Father and Mother missing the treat – the film was *On Moonlight Bay* starring Doris Day. We staggered out, drunk with pleasure, into the middle of the night. But there was more: Bee bought us chips on the way home. Drizzle was making haloes around the street lights. We had seen Doris Day, and our choice of favourite film star, and our ownership of cigarette cards was vindicated; we were real people, with lips and fingers stinging with salt and vinegar.

'What the bloody hell time of night do you call this?'

Father was waiting in the hall, wearing a sleeveless pullover and pyjama trousers, waving the alarm clock.

The house seemed dark when we got home from school the

next day. It was cold. Mother was kneeling in front of the fire trying to blaze up the wet coal with a newspaper. She had cut her finger on the bread knife and a thick drop of blood splashed onto the tiled fireplace. She was crying. Bee had gone.

Suzannah and Maria are still with us, as reminders of Auntie Bee, in a manner of speaking. You see, their heads and limbs were attached to their bodies with elastic bands and over the years they had many adventures, until somehow there were just enough parts to make up one doll. We call her Zan-Mri now. It does seem a shame that Auntie Bee, who gave her to us, never married. She was wonderful with children.

As she leaves the office Catriona Ling swallows two Quiet Life tablets and drops her paper cup into a wastebin full of crumpled paper and cigarette butts. She is feeling sick with the apprehension that curdles her life like sour milk. Bee, she remembers, used to smoke some exotic brand, De Reszke or Du Maurier or Black Cat, screwing a cigarette into a green and black holder banded in marcasite with her red-tipped nails, leaning to flick her lighter at Mother's Woodbine. Catriona wishes that she had not lost the deco cigarette case that somebody once gave her, because it is important that she appear to be a success. She is afraid that she will regress to a four-year-old, blurting out her troubles to Bee. She is regretting her impulse to telephone her, worried about her choice of restaurant, which, convenient for her, will mean that Bee will probably have to take taxis. Anxiety buzzes away, under the grief of a recent bereavement; there is her old uncle, her father's only surviving brother, for whom Catriona has somehow become responsible; the women's publishing co-operative in which she is a partner is in dire financial straits; there are friends in hospital she should be visiting; calls she is too tired and dispirited to return when she gets home in the evenings; the heating in her flat is on the blink, ready to fail at the first really cold weather; the hoover is broken; the mortgage huge; the car due for a service; her cat is on tablets, hence the scratches on her hands; and her lover, Rachel, has volunteered to take part in a late night television programme where unattractive people talk frankly about their sexual practices. And she had meant to have her hair cut before seeing Bee.

A wind whips her across Covent Garden, and the sight of people bedded down in doorways does not make her count her blessings; instead the dark shapes are absorbed into her despair. At least she has arrived before Bee, but her relief is swamped by terror that she has got the wrong place, the wrong time. Noise bounces off the tiled walls as she sips a glass of wine and she knows that she should have chosen somewhere more *intime*. But for what? To tell Bee that she was sorry that they hadn't invited her to Mother's funeral? To say that she, Catriona, had never forgotten the first sight of Bee swinging along the road, of her turbaned head, and houndstooth jacket flaring from padded shoulders, her red lipsticked mouth, and wide black trousers skimming thick high-heeled black suede shoes? To mumble how Bee's risky glamour set her above the respectable overalled neighbours and teachers with their hair in buns like dried figs, and that she had always had a thing about trouser ladies? Or to confess how, later, any old collar-and-tie hunched over a pint of Guinness would set her young heart racing, as if one of those pinstriped pockets held the key to the world she was desperate to enter, and how, in her teens, she had lurked outside clubs, not daring to ask anybody to take her in? Should she risk confiding that only she, of all the family, could guess what hell that visit to Canterbury had been for Bee? Then she sees Bee, walking a bit stiffly, leaning on a silver-topped cane, being led by a waiter towards her table.

Bee, treading carefully so as not to slip on the floor which feels like an ice-rink as pain flares around her hip joints, has a sudden memory of Alec slamming down his miner's helmet with its lamp on the kitchen table, and his snap tin and dudley

– metal lunch box and water bottle – in hard, shiny, male challenge to her, and sees his eyes glaring out of the grimy face, which he has left unwashed, and the blue coal-dust scars under the skin of his arms. And Betty is standing up and waving to her across the restaurant, the light catching that red, crinkle-crankle, zig-zag, rick-rack hair; except that it is Catriona, of course, who is kissing her awkwardly on both cheeks now, bumping her nose.

Bee hadn't meant to say it so soon, but putting down her glass, while they are waiting for the starters, she hears herself. 'I was rather puzzled – and very upset to tell the truth – to get a birthday card from the twins. Signed by them both. When, you know, you told me the sad news on the telephone – that Erica has died. I didn't know what to think. I'm sorry, I didn't mean to upset *you*, my dear . . .'

'No, it's all right. I mean, it isn't really at all. But you haven't upset me. It's difficult to explain. We're all upset. Donald and Jamie and their families, but you remember how the twins were always a bit – odd. Different. They never – I mean, I don't suppose you recall those dolls – well, anyway, over the years they, Heather and Erica, sort of – amalgamated. As far as Erica's, I mean, Heather's concerned, they're both still there, nothing has changed. So we go along with it . . .'

Catriona is looking helplessly at Bee when the food arrives. Neither of them wants it.

'Are they still mad about Doris Day?' Bee asks resolutely, dipping a bit of bread into olive oil.

'Oh yes!'

In fact, Catriona and Rachel have a tape of Doris Day's Greatest Hits, which they like to play full blast in the car. She doesn't tell Bee how Father took them all to see *By the Light of the Silvery Moon*, the sequel to *On Moonlight Bay*, a couple of years after Bee's flight from Canterbury, or tell her how she and Mother had wept, each for her own reasons, while watching *Calamity Jane* on television, not long before Mother died, or say that the scene where Calamity and Adelaide Adams transform Calam's filthy cabin into a pretty love-nest for two always breaks her heart. 'A woman and a whisk broom can accomplish so much. Never underestimate a woman's touch!' The film should have ended there, with the two of them so obviously in love. Catriona resolves to try to put the romance back into her marriage when she gets home tonight by the light of the silvery moon. Then, aware that a long silence is hanging over their table in the clamour all around them, she looks up.

Bee, the birthday girl, is raising her glass in salute, smiling across glistening strips of red and yellow peppers on painted plates, saying, 'This is fun!' and she sees that Bee, the good old trouper, is going to make the evening all right.

Heartsease

HANAN AL-SHAYKH
Translated from the Arabic
by Catherine Cobham

THE SILVER rays cast by the full moon over the village of Kaukaban were unusually bright because the village was higher even than the clouds. It appeared to have grown by itself on the summit of the mountain for how could the clay and earth and little coloured glass windows have been transported up there unless a goat had carried them in its teeth? And even a goat would have needed some kind of track; a human being, without shoes or sandals, could never have done it. All the same the village was there, carved into the rocky mountain, making the summit into a complete circle. It was as if the mountain had enlisted the help of jinns to build a place which was so inaccessible that only those who loved it would make the effort to reach it. Every stone was polished and arranged with regard to its size and colour and the result was an ornament of incomparable beauty.

When the moon was full the women were overcome with happiness, eagerly anticipating the things they would do – fill the paraffin lamps, and stay up late strolling around well into the night now that they no longer needed to be afraid of scorpions and snakes. They would set off to listen to songs and chew qat in the yards of their mud brick houses, accompanying each other on drums and tambourines, all happy except Layla who used to say, 'Every time there's a full moon, it reminds me that life is short.'

But the village women who practised magic were convinced that the silver moonlight spoilt their witchcraft and waited until the moon had waned or was completely hidden by the clouds before they began again to prepare amulets, which were always written under cover of darkness, or bury locks off doors in the night (this was done to open up a woman's tubes). The moonlight not only laid bare their plans and destroyed their potions but seemed to exert its authority over all human powers. Only the woman known as Heartsease was different: she swore she could only work magic by moonlight. She always claimed that its silver beams penetrated curtains, stonework, wood shutters and glass windows and shook her awake if she was asleep, jolted her into action if she was still, made her get to her feet if she was sitting down. It also gave her the power to see beyond the field and the hills and the villages on the plains below to take in the whole country at a glance.

This time they didn't believe her. They knew that exaggeration was the breath of life to her, but they had faith in her ability to see into the unknown, prepare love and hate potions, compose prayers to retrieve lost articles, obtain God's mercy, divert plotters and schemers, make fruit grow bigger, get rid of ants, make a woman beloved by the man she desired, provide a woman with a mirror to reflect the inner thoughts of those who wished her ill, especially a mother-in-law or a co-wife. She even made up special prayers for backbones so that they were not burdened with too many heavy loads. She could make hair grow, stop the stomach demanding more food and, most important of all, compose prayers to awaken passion in husbands so that they came home for a visit, and in bachelors so they thought about marriage. They knew her ability to alter feelings and intentions, for she had been on the verge of reducing Raifa's husband to a pair of lusting eyes and a prick panting like an asthmatic chest. But Raifa had chickened out at the last moment and had given the potion, made of a sheet of red ink scribblings soaked in herbs and water, to her nanny goat instead of putting it in her husband's coffee. After that the goat followed Raifa wherever she went, snuffling at the hem of her dress and bleating incessantly to attract her attention. Its excitement reached a peak whenever Raifa bent over or squatted on her haunches as she worked in the field and around the house.

Eventually Raifa lost patience and started running away from the goat or throwing lettuce seeds over it to break the spell, vowing even to put up with her husband. But all her efforts did nothing to curb the goat's lust and in the end her husband, who knew nothing of all this, became convinced that the goat was ill and this was its way of complaining or saying goodbye to its owners. And so one morning he slaughtered it and skinned it and was amazed to see how enlarged its heart was.

However, the women felt sorry for Heartsease because she was over thirty and not yet married. They knew why she had refused many offers for she and her cousin had been in love, but he had gone and married someone from another village and no longer dared visit Kaukaban.

One day when the women were joking that Heartsease had missed the boat, she invited them to come and see the dozens of suitors from their village and villages round about who were asking for her hand. The hopeful suitors stood one after another in front of the closed door, which she refused to open. Afterwards the women flocked around her, demanding to know why she had rejected them, and she told them that she didn't want a man who was bewitched. 'If he embraced me, it would be because I wanted him to. The same if he talked to me or slept beside me. Everything he did would be because I'd decided he should, except going to the bathroom.' Then she reconsidered and said, 'Even that could be because I wanted him to. Perhaps if I was busy and wanted him out from under my feet for a bit.'

Time went by and Heartsease did not appear to suffer from being unmarried, in fact quite the contrary. She made it plain that she was happy, saying, 'I'm free, comfortably off. I'm Heartsease, not a beast of burden carrying some man's kids. What's more, marriage stops you feeling feminine and changes the love inside you into children. Your back's killing you from working in the fields and your husband's sitting there calling out, "Where's my dinner? Where's my qat?" You find you're always trying to snatch a bit of time to go and chat with your friends.'

Not content with making comments like these, she would always show her annoyance when she heard of someone getting married or having children – her lip curling with distaste, she would gesture towards her stomach and her breasts and say, 'Breast feeding. All that milk. It's disgusting.'

Her hair was parted in the middle, shiny black with not a trace of grey, not even disguised with henna. She wore coral beads round her neck, and what was astonishing about her was that she was always beautifully adorned. She put kohl round her eyes, one of which was black and one brown, her headdress was made of material which gleamed like stars and her perfume was a costly essence which she had bought on her travels, mixed with rose water. To make it penetrate the fabric of her clothes thread by thread and never fade, she had constructed a circular stand for her dress out of tree branches and she kept a lighted incense burner under it all night. The other women came to her from daybreak onwards and always found her without a hair out of place. When they commented on this, she remarked that she was never alone: if there weren't human beings with her, there were always external forces which she couldn't give a name to. 'Jinns?' they asked.

'I don't know,' she answered, 'but I have conversations with them, so they must be present and able to see me, even if it's only in my mind, so why shouldn't I look as nice as possible for them? Anyway it makes me stronger and more self-confident.'

The moon was full that night. Dogs howled and chased it as it raced from one mountain top to another. It looked as if you could reach out and touch it, a flat loaf browning in the oven, or half a melon. The custom was that the moment you saw the full moon, you made a secret wish and then kissed the one you were with. So the women kissed each other on the cheeks, saying basmallas and making wishes, especially for the crops to ripen in their fields. Then they went on their way in and out of alleyways, under arches, across the open ground between the houses to see Batul whose husband had been buried exactly a week before. The old women began to hand out advice, telling Batul not to look at the moon because it was male and the angels might drop her husband's soul as they headed through the skies towards Paradise. Then as the time passed they all forgot their well-tried sayings and pieces of advice, the widow and her grief slipped their minds and unawares they began stealing glances at the moon and the stars through the open window, which brought comfort to their hearts. They were enjoying the view without having to move their bodies, exhausted by the day's work, slumped loosely under their black velvet embroidered dresses with gold and silver belts slung round the hips.

All the women of the village were there except the young girls who roamed the hills and rooftops as usual, and visited each other's houses, trailed by dogs and younger sisters. Their voices could be heard recriminating, scolding, sometimes laughing, carried by the dry, clear air to the crowd of women in Batul's house.

The gap created by the absence of Heartsease was tangible: she was the last bead in the rosary and her presence pulled the other beads together and completed the string. Everything she said aroused the enthusiasm and interest of the others, even though they did not always agree with her. She had been the first to look into the unknown and see oil under the rocks and fields in many different places, and then see Saudi Arabia shaking a finger at foreign oil companies, warning them not to look for oil in Yemen; for it wanted to be the only country with oil so that the Yemenis would not stop working there. She had been right and now the villages were like bags emptied of their contents and thrown to one side, as if war had broken out and all the men had been called up. This was what had happened: the men had abandoned their dark shops, which were no more than wooden cupboards, to go and work in Saudi Arabia, leaving the villages to the women. They visited their families once a year when strings of taxis would arrive from the airport loaded with televisions, videos and blankets. This would go on until they came to the end of their active lives and prepared to face old age and the hereafter by returning home for the last time. They failed to notice that their women had changed completely, even in their choice of vocabulary, and had a special language of their own.

When time passed and still Heartsease did not join the gathering to offer her condolences to Batul, one of the women went out to the edge of the porch and called her name at the top of her voice. This was the way people normally hailed each other, or had arguments, or announced news, good or bad. But Heartsease did not appear or call back to explain or apologise. Although the evening passed off satisfactorily without her, they became increasingly anxious. Some of them were more curious than worried and their curiosity was tinged with jealousy. Whatever was stopping her coming must certainly be important, otherwise how could she stay away from an occasion like this? It would become a stain on her past along with her other idiosyncracy – the habit she had of going off on trips by herself from time to time, which harmed her reputation, especially as she used to come back exhausted, vague and depressed, then shut herself up and listen to strange music which she had brought with her.

The moment they had said goodbye to Batul they hurried off, and, as if by unspoken agreement, went over the rocks and hillocks and along the twisting lanes to the house where Heartsease lived. There was no light from inside but the outside was lit up by the moon. They shouted at her, reproaching her for not coming, banged on her door, threw little stones at the wooden shutters, but there was no response. They repeated the onslaught once, twice, three times and finally heard her voice asking them to go away because she was working and didn't want to be disturbed, didn't want anything to spoil her concentration. One of them replied derisively, 'So you think you're the governor!'

The others laughed for in the next village the children had been obliged to stop playing in their normal rowdy groups at siesta time for a whole month while the provincial governor was visiting his family.

At this Heartsease opened the window and whispered, 'Have you forgotten that there's a full moon above your heads! Leave me alone now and come back tomorrow morning. I promise you, your hair will go white with shock!'

They did not believe her. She must have remembered the gathering at Batul's only after she had removed her headdress. Or perhaps she just had not looked as beautiful as she would have liked to. Sometimes she found herself pretty and sometimes really ugly, especially before her period when she used to say that everything swelled up, even her beauty spot, even the little hairs in her eyebrows.

They started shouting again. Laughing, they reminded her of the story of Layla and the monkey shit. They still remembered how some of the magic she had attempted when the moon was full had failed. She had asked Layla to bring her some monkey's faeces. Layla's husband had just married another wife, years younger than Layla, and the idea was that when his glance fell on the bewitched faeces and then on his new wife she would seem drab and ugly and give off a smell of shit.

But when he came home and took his new wife in his arms, delighted because she was pregnant less than a month after their marriage, Layla was sure he hadn't even noticed the stuff. She tried putting it somewhere more conspicuous and her husband simply remarked that it was the faeces of an animal not found in the village. She conveyed this information to Heartsease, who would not believe that she had failed but would only concede that the shit must have been bogus. In any case, how could Layla have procured it, when a snowfall was just about as likely as a monkey in this village! She didn't believe that Layla had hitched a ride with a medical mission that had passed through the village one day and gone to Taiz where there was a cage full of monkeys by the museum gateway. She accused her of lying and told everyone who intervened to confirm that Layla was telling the truth that they were hypocrites. A few days later Layla returned accompanied by a procession of children, old people and youths, all eager to tell Heartsease about the monkey Layla had bought with the proceeds from her gold jewellery. Heartsease came to examine the monkey and was delighted. She had never seen one before. Its small searching eyes pleased her and she muttered that at last she understood the secret of the magic hidden in its eyes. Those who heard what she said were afraid that she might demand its eyes for her witchcraft, but she asked to be left alone with it, then came out and told Layla that the shit had to be black. But Layla's husband took his second wife in his arms again, curious to know the identity of the strange beast that had emptied its bowels in front of his house, in case its flesh was good to eat. Heartsease claimed again that the shit was not black enough and the whole village went on trying to think of some food which would make it really black, without much success. Eventually the story leaked out through the women and children, Layla's husband came to hear of it and went crazy because his wife had spent so much money and sold her jewellery for the sake of some monkey shit. He swore he would take a third wife and so he did.

The women started shouting again, calling to Heartsease to show herself. In the end her scowling face appeared at the window. She warned them to keep away from her house and respect what she was trying to achieve on this momentous night, promising that she would show them the results in the morning.

With one accord, they retreated a few steps in silence, then returned as if bewitched to their places in front of the house. The moon was shining directly above it. They were happy with the night, despite their grief over the dead man and his widow. Their visit to Batul had actually made them content and grateful and they praised the Lord that their husbands were still in the land of the living, not in the next world like Batul's, especially since he'd died in Saudi Arabia and she'd had to pay for the transportation of the body and its burial here in the village. What's more, his wages had stopped and from now on she'd have to rely solely on what she grew in the field. This death in the village reminded them how lucky they were, brought it home to them that they were married, yet free.

So wide were their eyes with sleeplessness that they seemed to fill the whole of their faces. The women appeared confused, circling round the house, sitting down, standing up. They were convinced that vibrations given off by Heartsease had drawn them here, with the intervention of the moon. It was said that people had walked on the moon. At the time the village sheikh had broadcast from the minaret that a cow must be slaughtered to atone for the moon's defilement.

They would have remained under the sway of Heartsease and their own euphoria had they not heard the voice of the billy goat. 'We've even woken the goat,' remarked Raifa. Then she sang a song that came into her head at that moment:

> Come my love and see
> I've bought you some qat
> Feed it to that little bird
> And he'll become a billy goat with horns

When they turned instinctively to look at Heartsease's goat as if awaiting its reaction to Raifa's song, they found that it was not in its usual spot.

They went all around the outside of the house looking for it, convinced that Heartsease had forgotten to tie it up and that it was wandering alone in the mountains. They were a little worried about it but their concern led to much hilarity as Raifa imitated the goat leaping high in the air when the dogs nipped its hindquarters, which was what had happened to Wajiha's donkey. Raifa started calling Heartsease, telling her that her goat had escaped and was lost, but instead of Heartsease answering, the goat bleated and the sound came from inside the house. At this the women's confusion mounted, clouding their vision. It was this confusion which led Raifa to call out once, twice, three times, asking Heartsease about the goat, until at last they heard her voice shout back insolently, 'Now do you believe me? The goat's with me. That should prove to you that I'm absorbed in my work.'

They went back to their homes and the sound of their snoring rose in the air as soon as they threw themselves on to cushions in their living rooms, too tired even to put down their mattresses. The next day they brought their bread to the oven to bake as they did every morning, milked the sheep, collected the eggs, then prepared coffee with ginger before hurrying off to the field which was swathed in mist as it was every morning. When they met Heartsease at the pond with her goat drinking at her side, they asked her where she had found it, flatly refusing to acknowledge her claims of the previous night. As if she understood, she too acted as if nothing had happened and contented herself with patting the goat's neck, stroking its horns, brushing some specks of mud off its coat and waving a fly away from its eyes. Ignoring this pantomime, they continued with their efforts to catch her out, and asked her why she had not turned up to visit Batul. She answered them with a huge ringing laugh, throwing her head back so that all her teeth and her uvula were on show. Then she began to tell them about the silver light of the moon, but the women did not listen. They walked away from her in exasperation and went to work in the field which lay in the valley, and which they had planted with walnut trees, qat, wheat, fenugreek and vegetables. It was as if the subject of Heartsease no longer had any significance since the events of the night before. They put all their efforts into their toil under the burning sun, singing together or letting one woman sing alone to break up the day's monotony, amusing themselves by talking to the animals that helped them with ploughing and carrying, studying the position of the sun and clouds, examining each other's crops and muttering basmallas to ward off the evil eye.

That night Heartsease's goat disappeared again and she shut herself away as she had done before. This might have been forgotten within a few days if the goat had not appeared the next morning streaked with henna. Layla examined it and informed the other women that it had a different look in its eyes from before. The women did not enquire further or comment on the goat's transformation. Instead they increased the number of basmallas they said when they found themselves face to face with Heartsease or caught her looking in their direction. They had instructed their children from an early age to say 'God protect us' to themselves whenever she came in sight.

When the goat disappeared and Heartsease shut herself away for the third night in a row, Layla and Raifa hurried to her house. They had been delegated by the others to go alone as it would have made too much noise had they all gone. They searched for traces of the goat, keeping their movements so restrained that not even a small exhalation of breath escaped their lips. They clung unblinking to the wall hour after hour until they heard the goat making a commotion inside the house as if it was kicking its hooves against something. Minutes went by. Nothing but silence and waiting. Raifa looked at Layla as if she hoped she too was having second thoughts about being there. When Layla did not respond, Raifa motioned with her head that they should leave. Layla moved her head slowly from side to side in a gesture of refusal, then looked in front of her, making her eyes soft as if begging her companion to be patient. Silence. Silence. Silence and then the sound of a throat being cleared in the still air, deafening them and making their hearts stop beating. It was not Heartsease or any other woman, nor the goat or any other animal. Was it a spirit? Then there was Heartsease saying, 'Bless you.'

The two women shook their heads in horror. Heartsease would never talk to a spirit in such a homely way, as if she was sitting beside it. Confusion, fantasy, conjecture and logic mingled wildly in their heads, and without saying anything they slipped away back to the others to receive confirmation and reassurance that they were still sane, for they were picturing the strangest scenes and believing in them without much hesitation. They were like bats using sound vibrations to construct a detailed image of their prey and its whereabouts.

They pictured that Heartsease had changed the man she loved into a goat – for she had sworn when news of his marriage reached her that she would have her revenge on him even if it took years. They also pictured that she had managed to change the goat into a man who was a replica of her beloved. Then they reverted to the first version and decided that, having bewitched him, she had forgiven him and turned him back into a man, or that she had tried before and had succeeded only in the past three days, or that she was still in the process of bewitching him. Was the village not already familiar with the story of the magician who used to turn her lover into a donkey in the day and back into a man at night, all to avoid the talk and the violence of the men in her family, since her lover was from another tribe?

There was no other explanation, for even though the two women had been certain that it was a man they heard coughing, there was nowhere in the village she could have found one. In the tombs? In the photographs in pride of place on living room walls? In the worn clothes left hanging on a nail because the men had to be dressed in their best when they went away to work? In their voices sent to their families on cassettes because they didn't know how to write and their women didn't know how to read? There was no trace of them there except in memories, and can a memory give birth to a man of flesh and bone?

So the two women slipped away from Heartsease's house like hairs from flour and gradually fear began to take a hold of them, despite their curiosity and the shock of discovery, and they repeated basmallas and recited the prayer to drive away fear, only to ask God's forgiveness again for it was a prayer composed by Heartsease.

The village rapidly became like a green melon being tapped to find out if it was red and sweet-tasting inside. Layla's daughter was the only one to remind them that Heartsease had tried to explain what was really going on when they asked about the goat. As soon as she had begun talking about the silver moon and the way it worked miracles for her they had walked off. The women listened to Layla's daughter for a moment, then went back to their noisy debate. They wished there was just one man in the village, somebody's husband or brother whom they could consult. They had wished this often before, when one of the children or animals became ill, or the traps they set for the birds that ate the seeds failed to work.

Then they said they wished their village was close to the other villages, instead of being up in the clouds, so they could seek help from a man of religion. The fact that the mosque had no Quran reciter and no muezzin must mean that there was a way in for magic to interfere with religious belief. Then once more they blamed the location of their village – the influence of the moonlight must be twice as strong as in other villages.

They thought again about hiding from the moon, out of range of its bright beams, but quickly put the thought out of their minds, not wanting to hasten an eclipse and bring bad luck on themselves. All these fantasies were little more than ruses to dull the persistent notion that they must see what was really going on in Heartsease's house.

So moving forward like a column of black ants, their black shawls covering their heads, their black dresses raised so they would not impede their progress and the arches of their dry feet hardly touching the ground, they passed through the main gate in the wall and on through the other entrances so they could go to her by the rocky track beyond the village. Then if the dogs howled and Heartsease looked out she would see no trace of them. They went by the pond and the moonlight made the green moss on the water's surface look like strange insects. Then they encircled Heartsease's house, which fitted into the circumference of the mountain, like a silkworm wrapping itself round a mulberry leaf. The dark windows surrounded by white plaster looked like watching eyes.

The sight of the closed door and the high windows discouraged them but then a light shone suddenly in a window, their eyes fell on the goat's empty patch and they felt a renewed surge of curiosity about what was taking place in the house.

Each woman had a different image of what she was going to see inside: a goatskin lying on the floor and the man whom Heartsease had loved standing there as large as life imploring her to turn him back into a man for good, kissing her feet contritely; a man's head on a goat's body or the other way round; a goat begging her not to turn it back into a human being because it did not like dealing with mankind: 'I've had enough of their evil ways. Especially yours.'

Their curiosity rose to delirium, increasing their strength and eagerness, and they formed a pyramid, each on another's shoulders, until Raifa reached the window and saw the lamp lighting up the room. But it was really the moon which illuminated the room, making it as bright as day, so that Raifa could see Heartsease lying on her side, smoking a cigarette, her hair spread out around her. Most of her flesh was exposed and beside her was the man who had brought back the body of Batul's husband.

Hey Diddle Diddle!

GILLIAN HANSCOMBE
AND SUNITI NAMJOSHI

Hey, diddle, diddle,
The cat and the fiddle,
The women chased after the moon;
La Belle Dame laughed
To see such fun,
And I ran away with the spoon.

THE GURU has no interest in uniformity; we are, after all, individualists here, but she does set certain standards. My problem is that these standards are encoded, they are veiled and embodied, they are intertwined in ritual. And I am not a poet. For me, a metaphor is *not* as good as a mouthful. I want paraphrase, not poetry, as Margot once put it. Was she being sarcastic? I want the truth; well, a truth, I mean something I can explain in a clear and concise manner to anyone else who might want to know.

For example, in the mornings, to greet the sun, the guru wraps herself in green. (Why green? She is consistent, though problems arise when the greens merge into blues and yellows. I have never as yet ventured to say so, but surely, in almost any

145

universe precision does matter?) She has both rich fabrics and plain, brocades, silks, weaves and cottons, in every shade of emerald, jade, lime and olive. She breathes out slowly on plants and trees, on food and drink, and on all of us. (But what does she breathe in? The morning air? The green of the trees? And what precisely is the effect on her?)

Then at noon she has lengths of scarlet in a range of styles: togas, saris, cassocks, caftans, sarongs. (Don't the styles matter? Surely, consistency is important in any universe. I have not, as yet ventured . . .) She plays music, we dance or listen. We each have a small bell of bronze or brass which suspends from the middle right-hand finger. (Some consistency there. When Margot lost hers, I went to considerable trouble to find it for her.)

At dusk the guru wears blue, for the closing sky, the waiting sea, the ribbons of river and creek, which are our focus before eating. (This is the bit that makes me most uneasy. How focus on emptiness? It allows a certain latitude. It has crossed my mind that the guru is simply a woman who adores nice clothes. But a wise woman who is fond of fashion? Not quite adequate. And yet, surely explanation and explication are useful in any universe?) After eating we sleep.

It's an easy life, given the alternatives. Everything is permitted except moonworship, which is her prerogative, having been chosen. And the talking cat, of course. (The talking cat is not fictitious. She converses with me – occasionally – in polysayables. I perceive that her sentences are formed, her grammar impeccable. The problem is that I'm not altogether sure what she is saying. She is not poetic, but the bits of information she – occasionally – proffers, just lie in my mind like pieces of a landscape, though for her, no doubt, they have a life of their own, and all rise up and fit together in a constant movement, forming, as it were, pattern upon pattern. This was a dream I had about the talking cat and her jigsaw puzzle. I did not write it down. It seemed too fanciful.) The rest of us wonder and meditate. We never discuss it, not all together, anyway. We're only learning, after all.

It's a quiet life, but that's what we asked for. The world was too ambitious, the men too warlike, the women too wifelike, the children too wise too soon; and the computers knew too much.

My best friend here is officially Martha, but my favourite is Margot, who has no friends because of her three eyes, which frighten people, though we all hope one day to be free. Fear is addictive, says the guru, and we all agree.

Margot collects everyone's dreams and illustrates them in books she makes herself. She can draw, paint, draft, and design. She makes collages and experiments with photographs. Once in every lunar month, Margot gives her books to the talking cat, who scrutinises them carefully. Then the guru shelves them in the second library. None of us minds; the dreams keep Margot's eyes on her work. The guru says it's the cleanest thing to do.

Margot is the only one of us who never argues, though she obviously has her own thoughts about everything. Once, for example, I saw her hugging the trees, kissing them, and I heard her telling them she was sorry they couldn't understand, but that purity was like that. (I like Margot. I think I like Margot, but she doesn't look at me. Sometimes I wonder what would happen to me if she were to bathe me in the full glare of her third eye; but that would be a foolishness I have not ventured to broach with her.)

When we were in the world we sacrificed for the sake of growth or change – for family, in some instances, or for revolution. Now we give up nothing at all. The guru says growth and change are circumstantial. Look at the talking cat, she reminds us.

History is in the first library, open in the afternoons. Martha and I cook a lot together, but the rest of the time we mostly spend in the first library. Neither of us is so keen on the second library; that's where the poetry is, and all the reminiscences, including our own. Martha and I want to master the history of the world so we can see how things ended up this way. The guru laughs at us; she says it's perfectly obvious how – and why; but Martha and I remain unconvinced. In any case, we don't want to spend our time in the second library. When I first came, I argued a lot with the guru. What if there's something we haven't heard of, or haven't thought of? For example, I suggested; what exactly happens in the moonlight? What is significant about it? She didn't answer directly; she's a great one for telling stories, by way of explanation, but I'm sure I never get the proper meaning. Nor does Martha. We're reduced, quite often, to telling the stories again, over and over, to each other, to see if the meaning becomes obvious; but it hardly ever does. It's no good asking her, either, for the real meanings. She only smiles and says some things are personal, in the end. I can't stop wondering, though. Nor can Martha. But since we've all promised not to look or listen, I can't see how we'll ever find out. (Everyone thinks Martha and I are best friends. Martha thinks so too. We are so alike, she says, so practical. I am not practical, I am theoretical, but, of course, I can't quite say that to her.)

I haven't, up till now, felt any particular connection myself to the moon, though there must be one, or what's all this for? The guru would say, if she were here, what's anything for? She can't hear me though; she's in the second library checking through the reminiscences for correlations and corroborations.

The talking cat has the third library, if you can call it that, given that there are no books there at all. There's only the computer, with a stack of CD Roms and a modem, all sound sensitised so she can operate everything vocally. The guru says cats have an overtone series which can work like our tone languages, so the talking cat can call up anything from anywhere: the British Library, the Library of Congress, the Sorbonne, the UN databases. None of us understands why she wants to key into such things, but we respect her individuality, and she is an extremely intelligent cat, so it must mean something. (I once begged the cat to key in the moon into all the databases in all the world. She blinked at me and complied. The computers would still be churning if I had not begged her once again to cancel the compilation. It was foolish of me. Precision is important, but then so is demarcation, not to mention deconstruction . . .)

What I'd really like to know is what the guru wears for the moon. (It has taken me a long time to formulate my question.) Every day I try to breathe through my curiosity, just as we breathe through pain, and memory, and everything else that's problematic. I haven't succeeded yet; but nor has Martha, so at least I'm not on my own. On the other hand, we both so much want to know that we don't dare tell each other how intense the desire is. That's another reason why we keep on with the history of the world. That's going to take a very long time, so it's a major distraction.

Recounting the obvious does give some relief. (Martha thinks it was her question. She even suggested that we ask the guru. It took me a long time to persuade her that that just wasn't done.) It can't, after all, be green, red, or blue, I tell Martha. And yellow wouldn't make sense at night. What about purple, we wonder, because it's regal; or white, for innocence. No, says Martha; and no, I agree; that's how things are in the world. It could be anything; it could even be black, since it's all her own construction – this place, this code, these rituals, these people.

We don't all change three times a day ourselves, though it's hard not to copy what she does, given her confidence. She's a mountain compared with us. Although she's kind and patient, we all understand that we're simply part of the scenery, or the weather. In her case, it's the permanence that makes the difference, since we'll all have to leave at some point, though no one's sure when, or how. It unsteadies you knowing that, however much you concentrate on your breathing. I don't want to think for a second about leaving till I know what she wears for the moon. (No, I honestly don't think I'm in love with her. How can a mouse be in love with the moon? Did I say that? And Martha isn't either. Martha isn't capable of being in love. Though I have to say here that she thinks she is, in love, I mean, with the mountain or the moon, I'm not sure which.)

There are twenty-five of us here at the moment, not counting the guru or the talking cat. (And are all of us in love? Despite the lack of uniformity? Despite the individualism?) There were over two thousand at one time, when there was still the newsletter and before the guru opened the bank accounts. That was before I came, or Martha; but Margot was here from the beginning. That's another reason why I like her so much; she knows how to keep secrets. She knows, as well, how to flatter the talking cat, who isn't friends with anyone, on the whole. The guru says the talking cat has important work to do, so she can't spend time on leisure and pleasure like the rest of us. She makes time for Margot, though. They must have a lot in common.

Today is new moon again, which we always mark with a round table discussion. The guru says she appreciates the problems we come across, since she's aware that we're having a lot of experiences that don't make sense. Remember two things, she suggests: first, that what makes sense is always relative. Ask Margot, she adds, knowing that we won't dare. Secondly, she explains, everything that exists does, in the end, make sense; it's simply a matter of noticing all the details, which takes a lot of practice. I feel she's staring deliberately at Martha and me and it tempts me to start a tantrum, but the talking cat raises an eyebrow at me and it makes me concentrate on control. Martha is braver – I can feel her staring back. Time's run out, though, and we begin the meditation. And then suddenly, Martha blurts it out, 'What does the guru wear for the moon?' I'm horrified. I pretend I'm meditating and haven't heard. The guru really is meditating. Margot's third eye is firmly closed. But Martha is in a state beyond all restraint. She appeals to the cat. 'Tell me about the guru and the moon!' And the cat, the cat hasn't understood *that this is the question*. She takes it casually. We hear her say, 'I've been doing crocodiles lately. I will tell you about the crocodile and the moon.' Margot's third eye opens wide. The other women give up meditating and settle down to listen. This isn't quite what I had bargained for, but I listen too. The guru is above and beyond it all. She isn't listening, but this doesn't seem to bother the cat. The story goes like this:

> When the crocodile fell in love with the moon, she immediately became a nocturnal animal. The nights she would spend courting the moon. 'Come down,' she would cry to the silent moon. 'Oh please come down.' On the whole the crocodile's prayers went unheard. The moon was concerned with other matters, but she was not averse to a little admiration, even from a crocodile; and so, once in a while, she would scatter her moonbeams on the crocodile's lake with a special indulgence. The crocodile noticed this. It fed her hopes. She would speed through the water with all the impetuosity of a lovesick animal, even though at her approach the moonbeams scattered. 'I am being teased,' she thought. 'Teased and tested. I must persevere.' She spent the daytime composing sonnet sequences and dozing in the sun. It was necessary to prepare for her nightly exertions. And as time went by the crocodile's sonnets began to improve. The moon, without really intending it, had proved to be an excellent muse. It seemed to the crocodile that the moon was fickle –

151

sometimes she disappeared; that the moon was haughty
– she shed no moonbeams and seemed distant; that the
moon was shy and hid behind a cloud; or that the moon
was kind and shone with such effulgence that it would
only be a matter of days now before she came down.
And because the crocodile suffered, there was always
the thought that the moon was cruel. But then the
crocodile would hasten to say to herself, 'That is
unworthy. The moon is chaste. I must learn to love
better.' And so it went on: the crocodile's vigils and the
crocodile's poems; and in time her poems became quite
famous. So that eventually when the crocodile died – at
a ripe old age – and researchers asked, 'What exactly
made the crocodile tick?' a variety of conjectures were
on offer. Indeed, even today, there is a controversy as to
which of three factors contributed most to the
crocodile's inspiration: the effects of the moon; the
workings of nature (either her own, or nature in
general); or the fact that the crocodile had ample leisure.
The crocodile herself would no doubt have said that the
moon and the stars, time and tide, the nature of
existence, in short, fate itself had conspired against her.

When the cat has finished, she stretches, yawns and begins washing herself. Margot says, 'Thank you.' But no one else says anything at all. In the familiar silence I understand everything that has been opaque for so long. What crocodiles wear – that's the thing: what crocodiles wear on a clear night in honour of the moon. The power to sway the world's tides, to hide the huntress from her enemies, to make an ordinary girl a rhymester or a queen – that's no mean achievement. But a crocodile's tears, even under moonlight – is that the secret of success?

Margot gathers up the talking cat and they close their eyes together. The guru goes to her private suite to prepare for her ritual. I signal to Martha. Tonight we'll break faith and watch for all we're worth. The world is wide and all her mysteries are somewhere half-remembered, half-recorded, by three-eyed Margot and the talking cat. The guru orders thought and organises ceremonial. The rest of us dream and desire.

When it's deep midnight, no noise, no wind, no stirring of any kind, Martha and I creep slowly towards the back of the building where the French doors lead to the walled garden. We say nothing, but feel each other's guilt being easily overtaken by the passion for truth. I remember, anyway, the guru's guidelines on guilt: a spurious emotion, an indulgence, a conditioned response. What use is guilt? the guru would question; who does it help? What can it change?

There's a hedge of holly, and beyond, a circle of rose plants set amid a flat clean lawn. Martha and I lie full-length on our bellies. She's not yet there. She'll come from the other side, from her private rooms at the other end of the house. The white moon looks sharp as a sickle, but I still don't feel any connection. Nor does Martha: I can tell.

When she comes across the grass she carries a flagon of dark wine, and a tall glass glittering. But she wears nothing at all. Her skin shines, topaz and amber; shines like the fresh pips at the heart of a loquat. She has oiled herself, but she wears nothing at all. Even her bronze bell has gone from her finger.

She performs no meditation, but writhes on the grass, languishing, moaning. She drinks wine; she runs her hands through her hair. After some time, when the wine is two-thirds gone, she talks at the moon. I mean that she lifts her face; but there is no singing or chanting – just her daily inflection. She says, as if she were shopping or talking to the bank manager:

If I croon, O moon,
You dissemble;
If I swoon, O moon,
You reassemble.

153

And next she says:

> *I suffer your chastity*
> *Because of your piety.*

And last she says:

> *You promised me meaning, and metamorphosis:*
> *I hold your image close to my breast;*
> *Make me a swan, a stone, a princess!*

She goes inside. Martha is shivering so violently from the cold that she can't say anything. We creep back indoors and head for the kitchen. Coffee and talk is essential.

Martha glows with admiration and wants my agreement. Such a beautiful gown, so sheer, so soft; something other than silk, but completely natural. And the colour: how could one describe it?

I let her talk. I'm confused, of course. What gown? What colour? Nor has Martha heard a word. She tells me how moved she was, how soothed, how reassured. Such silence, she tells me; such profound and perfect silence. And the stillness! To sit so long, with not a single muscle moving. We must emulate, Martha concludes: it's quite clear now – it's a matter of silence and absolute dedication. Speech is distraction, she declares. And from that moment on, she will not say one word – not to me, not to anyone, though we sit next day in the library, reading as usual.

I'm lost without Martha's conversation, though it's clear the moon has turned her head, so even if she spoke, it could never be the same. There's no one I can talk to. It would mean a confession, since we broke faith and watched.

At full moon the guru asks for me. I have no trepidation; we are all asked for, from time to time. It will be the ceremonial soup, I am perfectly certain: the ancient porcelain, the long-handled spoons, the solitary candle. The scene is tranquil, but the bell on her finger is very active: she gesticulates wildly as she speaks. I know you have seen what can never be told, she accuses. What, therefore, is your intention?

I have no defence, of course. But my pride is intact. You can build a lot on pride, even a future. I tell her my disillusion, my depression, my disappointment. I tell her she's no better than the rest of us. I tell her she cheats and lies. I tell her she has no right to lead us on. She replies that rights are a matter of expectation. We agree I must leave. We finish our soup. Margot and the cat are summoned as witnesses. I stare at Margot. Her third eye is a work of art, beautifully painted in greens and blues. The cat curls comfortably at the guru's feet. All I hear is a domestic purr.

Clearly the guru is done with me. She strokes the cat, who then makes an effort and jumps on her lap. They're engrossed in each other. Is that all? I don't like being ignored quite so blatantly. I turn on Margot. I give her fair warning. I say I'll be back when the truth is uncovered. There are plenty of libraries back in the world, I say defiantly. I can carry on just as well with other people's books; and who needs Martha when she won't say a word? And who needs a talking cat who stalks around as if she's above petty practicalities? And who needs a Margot whose caution prevents her from using whatever she pretends to know? And above all, I rage, who needs anyone, who promises the truth without ever giving it?

Who, returns Margot, suddenly surprising me, needs a schemer, a spoiler, a single-minded seeker? Who needs the faith of the fanatic? Who needs the truth?

I care no longer about the meaning; but I like the lift and lilt of her voice, of her strange appositions, of her peculiar confidence. In response to my admiration her third eye widens and winks. She picks up a long-handled spoon and presents it to me. As a souvenir, she breathes, a token, a talisman, a trinket, a treasure. The hollow spoon mirrors my face, it reflects the candle, the light of the moon. The cat and the guru are fast asleep. Margot is smiling. A wink and a nod? Good enough, I must believe, in any universe.

By the Light of the Silvery Moon

ZOË FAIRBAIRNS

I HAD a terrible night. I was twisting and turning and sweating and swearing as I wrestled with temptation and argued the toss with my better judgement.

I want to do it, I said. I can't resist.

You can resist and you must, my better judgement replied. You mustn't do it. Remember what happened last time.

Last time was last time, I said. It's different now. I'm a different person.

You are the same person you ever were, my better judgement said, the only difference being that you are happier and healthier because you've been sensible enough and strong-minded enough to give up what you are now proposing to resume.

With all this argy-bargy going on I wasn't expecting to get any sleep, but I did. I nodded off at about three o'clock and was awake again at half past five.

The struggle continued.

I never said I was giving it up for good, I pointed out. Just one day at a time. Isn't that what they say at Twelve Step groups?

It is, my better judgement conceded, but I don't think you've quite got the point. They give up one day at a time in order to give up for ever.

I only agreed to give it up because it was getting to be a problem for me, I said. I don't feel as if it's a problem any more.

It will always be a problem, my better judgement said.

You could argue, I said, trying another tack, that a fixation on total abstinence is as neurotic and harmful as the thing you're abstaining from.

YOU could argue the hind leg off a donkey, my better judgement retorted.

By now it was ten to six. With the newsagent and general store on the corner due to open at six, there was nothing to stop me getting what I needed.

Damn place, said my better judgement. If it must open at this hour, why can't it restrict itself to selling newspapers?

I wasn't listening. I was already out of bed.

My better judgement fell silent, assuming, I supposed, that since I had made up my mind, there was no point in arguing with me. But I didn't feel as if I had made up my mind. That's much too decisive an expression for what I was feeling. I seemed to be in the grip of something stronger than myself.

That's what you have to do at Twelve Step groups, or so I've heard. Admit that there's something stronger than yourself and that it has you by the throat. Certainly true in my case. This one's need was so urgent that it wouldn't even let me get dressed properly. I dug a grubby T-shirt and track suit bottoms out of the laundry, threw them on, picked up my purse and dashed out of the flat.

Half-way down the stairs, I thought I was going to have a heart attack. There was this loud, rapid pulse banging in my ears and I was trembling all over. I made myself slow down. I didn't want to collapse in the street.

Why not? said my better judgement heartlessly. Collapsing

in the street might be the best thing that ever happened to you. You'd be carted off to hospital and kept under supervision.

I went by the station. It was only ten past six, but already commuters were beginning to gather in readiness for being crammed on to trains.

Poor sods, I said.

What do you mean, poor sods? screamed my better judgement. One of those poor sods is supposed to be you.

Not yet, I said. I'm not due in till ten today. I've got hours.

Hours to render yourself unfit to go in at all, my better judgement sighed. What are you going to do – phone in sick, or forget about it altogether?

Neither, I replied. I'll be there on time. You'll see.

I arrived at the shop. Two boys were coming out with newspaper bags over their shoulders. One of them held the door for me. He smirked and said something to his friend. I didn't hear what it was but I was convinced it was about me. I was furious. What business was it of his? What business was it of anybody's? The man behind the counter was staring at me. I thought he and the newspaper boys would later compare notes about what I had bought. I decided to throw sand in their eyes by buying some other things as well. I went to the self-service shelves and picked up a loose-leaf writing pad, a pot of marmalade, a packet of sticking plasters, a large bag of cheese and onion crisps, a handful of different-coloured ballpoint pens, a carton of milk, a loaf of bread, a half-pound of butter, some After Eights, some chocolate digestives, a bag of frozen peas and some continental mayonnaise. I paid for everything, packed it in a carrier bag and walked out.

I was so impatient to get home and get started that I could hardly hold back from breaking into a trot. I reminded myself of the heart attack risk and walked at an even pace. If I collapsed now I would be found with my shopping on me. There would be no denying what I was planning to do.

As I passed the station, a train was arriving. People got on.

As I watched them I felt wistfulness curling in my heart. They were normal people who hadn't been out shopping in the early morning. Most of them weren't even properly awake yet.

Not one of them was wearing a T-shirt or track suit bottoms. Not one of them looked as if they were locked in conflict with their better judgement or in thrall to an awful, irresistible urge. They had no plans for the next thirty minutes except to sit very still and read the paper. The strongest force in their lives was the train taking them to work. Once there, they would have a cup of coffee and gradually come to. They would chat to their friends and do whatever they were paid to do. Even if they were prey to shameful unnameable desires, office routine would hold them in check.

My bag brushed my leg, making my hairs stand on end. My better judgement was fighting a rearguard action. It's still not too late, it said. You haven't actually started yet. Just deposit your bag in the nearest rubbish bin and go for a nice walk in the park.

I'm not ditching my shopping, I said. I've paid for it.

If it's the money you're worried about, said my better judgement, get Silver Moon and Virago to reimburse you. This is all their fault.

How do you work that out? I said.

Suppose you had a friend with an eating disorder, said my better judgement.

Why should I suppose any such thing? I asked.

The better to understand what I'm telling you, said my better judgement patiently. After years of dieting and bingeing and feeling wretched, this friend has finally confronted her difficulty and taken herself in hand. She's stabilised her weight, learned to love her body, and adopted healthy eating patterns. What would you send her for her birthday? A catering size banana cream pie?

No, I said.

Of course you wouldn't, said my better judgement, and

neither would anyone at Silver Moon or Virago. They wouldn't send a bottle of gin to a recovering alcoholic either. So what made them think it was OK to write you a letter asking you to contribute to their anthology? They *know* you've been trying to give up writing.

I let myself into the flat and took my shopping into the kitchen. I dumped the bag on the table and peered inside. I was almost afraid to look, but there they were, nestling among the After Eights and the bread and marmalade and the mayonnaise and the frozen peas – the brand-new loose-leaf writing pad and the coloured pens.

I examined the pad first. I felt a sort of reverence as I drew it gently out of the bag. I held it close to my face and breathed in the faint chemical fragrance. It was a sexy smell and it aroused me. I turned back the cover and looked at the creamy expanse of the first page. I fingered the hard wiry spine and the perforations where the coils of wire gently but firmly penetrated the paper and held it in place, waiting for the first marks that I would set down on its pale, receiving surface.

Don't be afraid, I whispered softly. You and I are going to do amazing things together. You could be the first writing pad of the rest of my life.

Yeah, sneered my better judgement. You and all the others.

Don't interrupt, I said.

It's my duty to interrupt this nonsense, said my better judgement, before you spoil what remains of your mental balance, not to mention the rain forests.

Oh yes, I said, do let's bring the rain forests into this. Do let's be politically correct at all times.

My better judgement ignored me and went back to addressing my writing pad, talking to it about me as if I were not present.

She does this all the time, you know, it said, or at least she did until I convinced her that it wasn't getting her anywhere. Well, I thought I'd convinced her. I had high hopes that this job of hers might turn her into the sort of person for whom the fact that she hasn't got to be at work till ten means she'll stay in bed till nine. I thought she'd stop dashing out at the crack of dawn to procure stationery. I thought we were making progress, but that'll be straight down the toilet now, as will her job. No boss is going to tolerate an employee who doesn't turn up for work because some rash, unthinking acquaintance has asked her to write a story. Not even if the only reason the firm took her on in the first place was to fill up its disability quota. They'll go back to hiring nice reliable people in wheelchairs and give a wide berth in future to freaks with writing disorders.

That's what it'll come to. I'll lay any odds you like she won't go in to work today. Once she starts a story, the rest of the world can go hang.

Now this would be all very well, my better judgement continued, if there really was going to be a story at the end of it, but there won't be. Take my word for it. I know the routine. She'll write a page. Then she'll dismantle it, paragraph by paragraph. Next, she'll dismantle the paragraphs, sentence by sentence, phrase by phrase, word by word. She'll repeat this process for anything up to nine or ten hours. She's like those people who have to keep washing their hands. Their hands don't get any cleaner and she doesn't get any nearer to finishing a story. Eventually she'll stop but only because she's too tired and depressed to continue. Who wouldn't be tired and depressed after a day of dismantling paragraphs? Did I say a day? A day! Would that it were so! Anyone can make a fool of themselves for a day. But I've seen this go on for weeks. I've seen it go on for months – years, even.

Dismantled paragraphs are all she's got, you see. She hasn't got any stories. She thinks she has – that's part of the disorder – but she hasn't. She used to have some, but she's written them all. You'd think a person would accept that they'd written all their stories, wouldn't you? But she doesn't. She denies. She's denying now. She's kidding herself that she can write a story for the Silver Moon anthology. That's why you've been brought here, contrary to my wishes. I did get her to agree some time ago that it's not a very good idea to keep stationery in the house, particularly creamy, sexy writing pads like you which are her real weakness. Then Silver Moon and Virago have to come along and put their oar in. It's all very well for them, they don't have to live with her.

You do, though, don't you? But not for long. You can imagine the effect all her paragraph dismantling has on the likes of you. Why do you think she always goes for loose leaves and wiry spines? The better to rip you up, that's why. She's a proper little Jack the Ripper where loose leaf writing pads are concerned, as you will discover. And *you* needn't feel you're immune, my better judgement went on, peering into the shopping bag and addressing my new pens. She's just as bad with what she writes *with* as what she writes *on*. I won't even begin to tell you what she did to the word processor. Suffice it to say that malicious acts are specifically excluded from the guarantee and that's why we're back with old technology again. I'm sorry if I'm frightening you or shattering your illusions, said my better judgement, but I wouldn't want you to think that you're the first.

When my better judgement had finished haranguing my stationery, I looked at the clock. It was ten to seven, so I still had a good two hours before I needed to be out of the house.

I made myself a cup of coffee and carried it to my desk along with my new stationery which seemed to be trembling in my hands.

I sat down and slowly spread open the first page of the writing pad. I pulled the top off the first of the pens. Its ballpoint gleamed with sleek black ink. Very carefully I wrote the words 'By the Light of the Silvery Moon' at the top of the page. Then I stopped.

Now what happens? I said, but answer came there none.

What do I do next? I asked, a little more loudly.

Where are you? I cried.

Are you by any chance addressing me? my better judgement frostily enquired.

Oh you're still there, thank heaven for that, I said. I need you to tell me how to write this story.

At this, my better judgement finally lost its rag. Are you out of your MIND? it shrieked. Haven't you listened to a word I've said? Why should I help you to write this story? I don't WANT you to write this story. I don't want you to write ANY stories. I don't want you even to THINK about writing stories, ever again. That has been my position from the start. You have chosen to ignore it. WHY SHOULD I HELP YOU?

Because you're my better judgement, I wailed, and I can't write my story if you're against me.

Which just goes to show how wrong I can be. It is possible to write a story against one's better judgement. I have just done it. I think it's a story. I'm not sure. It's something. I haven't dismantled it. I haven't harmed my stationery whilst writing it – no more than stationery enjoys, anyway. And – in case you were wondering – I did get to the office on time.

I think my better judgement is secretly quite pleased. It won't admit it, of course. It won't come out of its sulk for a good while yet. Its nose has been pushed out of joint by my managing without it. Of course, it won't admit that either. It smiles thinly over my story and says, well, if you like this sort of thing, this is the sort of thing you will like – but you're not going to PUBLISH it, are you?

Notes on Contributors

HANAN AL-SHAYKH was born in 1945, brought up in Beirut and studied in Cairo and Beirut. She worked as a journalist for a leading Lebanese newspaper for a number of years, and now lives in London with her family. She has published two volumes of short stories and five novels in Arabic. Several of her short stories and two novels, *The Story of Zahra* and *Women of Sand and Myrrh* have been published in English translation; a third is being translated and will be published in 1995.

LISA ALTHER was born in Tennessee in 1944 and currently lives in Vermont and New York City. She has published four novels — *Kinflicks*, *Original Sins*, *Other Women*, and *Bedrock*. A novella called *Birdman and the Dancer* has just appeared in several European countries, and she is now completing her fifth novel, *Graveyard Love*. She has also written stories, articles and reviews for many American and English periodicals, and she has done readings and lectures throughout North America, western Europe, China, Australia, New Zealand, and Indonesia.

LIZA CODY is the author of the Anna Lee private detective series. She began her crime-writing career in 1980 when *Dupe* won Britain's John Creasey Memorial Prize for a first crime novel. It was also nominated for an Edgar Award by the Mystery Writers of America. Her latest novel, *Monkey Wrench*, has recently appeared. Her work, including Edgar and Anthony nominated short stories, has been published in over a dozen countries. Liza Cody was born and brought up in London and before becoming a full-time writer she was a student at the Royal Academy School of Art, a painter, a studio technician at Madame Tussauds and a graphic designer.

MERLE COLLINS is Grenadian. She has studied at the University of the West Indies, Georgetown University in the United States, and at the London School of Economics and Political Science. Her published work includes two volumes of poems, *Because the*

Dawn Breaks (1985) and *Rotten Pomerack* (Virago 1993), a novel, *Angel* (1987), *Watchers and Seekers: Creative Writing by Black Women in Britain* (edited with Rhonda Cobham, 1987) and a volume of short stories, *Rain Darling* (1990). Virago will publish her new novel, *The Colour of Forgetting*, in 1995. She is currently a lecturer in Caribbean Studies at the Polytechnic of North London. She lives in London.

FIONA COOPER was born in Bristol in 1955 and now lives in Northumberland, near the sea. She runs writing groups and workshops for women on Tyneside as well as experimenting with pottery, photography and tropical fish. She has written six novels: *Rotary Spokes, Heartbreak on the High Sierra, Not the Swiss Family Robinson, Jay Loves Lucy, The Empress of the Seven Oceans* and *Skyhook in the Midnight Sun* and one volume of short stories, *I Believe in Angels*. In addition she has contributed to numerous short story collections and writes articles for magazines, radio scripts and stand-up comedy.

ZOË FAIRBAIRNS describes herself as follows: she is 'secretly jealous of Fay Weldon, who has a whole shelf at Silver Moon devoted to her work. Zoë Fairbairns was hoping one day to fill a shelf of her own – with *Benefits, Stand We At Last, Here Today, Closing, Daddy's Girls* and whatever else might come along – but nothing has come along. She has been struck down by what some people call writer's block but what feels to her more like a sort of literary bulimia. She hopes to write more novels – in fact she has an idea at the moment – but she is not going to tempt providence by saying any more about it than that. In the meantime, she is going back to basics by re-reading Dickens, and working as a subtitler at the Independent Television Facilities Centre in West London.'

ELLEN GALFORD was born in New Jersey USA, came of age in New York City, and emigrated to Scotland in 1971. She has written four novels: *Moll Cutpurse: Her True History* (1984, reissued by Virago 1992); *The Fires of Bride* (1986); *Queendom Come* (Virago 1990); and *The Dyke and the Dybbuk* (Virago 1993). She lives in Edinburgh.

GILLIAN HANSCOMBE and SUNITI NAMJOSHI are long-time collaborators, as well as separately published poets. Their first joint work was *Flesh and Paper* (1986) and since then they have written various sequences and exchanges, culminating recently in *Kaliyug: Circles of Paradise*, a full-length lyrical satire commissioned by Pan Project Theatre Ensemble, London.

Gillian Hanscombe's most recent sequence is *Sybil: The Glide of Her Tongue*. Suniti Namjoshi's latest work is *Saint Suniti and the Dragon* (Virago 1994), published along with a reissue of her *Feminist Fables*.

Gilliam Hanscombe and Suniti Namjoshi live near Lyme Regis, Dorset.

ELIZABETH JOLLEY was born in England in 1923. Her first book, *The Five Acre Virgin and Other Stories*, appeared in 1976; since then she has published twelve books, among them the novels *Foxybaby*, *The Sugar Mother* and, most recently, *Cabin Fever* (1990), as well as a number of plays for radio. Her works have been translated into German, French, Spanish, and Russian; among her many honours she was the 1988 recipient of the Canada/Australia Literary Prize. She now lives in Western Australia where she teaches at the Curtin University of Technology, conducts writing workshops in remote country areas and in prisons, and raises geese and fruit trees on a small rural farm.

SHENA MACKAY has written seven novels, of which the latest *Dunedin*, won a Scottish Arts Council Award, and three volumes of short stories. She has also edited *Such Devoted Sisters* (Virago 1993), an anthology of stories about sisters. The *Collected Stories* and a new edition of the 1984 novel, *A Bowl of Cherries* has recently appeared. She lives in London.

SARA MAITLAND was born in 1950, brought up in Scotland and now lives in London. Her first novel, *Daughter of Jerusalem* won the Somerset Maugham Award in 1979. Her other novels include *Virgin Territory*, *Three Times Table* (all published by Virago), and *Home Truths*. She has also written several collections of short stories, the most recent of which is *Women Fly When Men Aren't*

Watching (Virago 1993); a book about women and Christianity, *A Map of the New Country* and a biography of Vesta Tilly (Virago 1986), star of the British music hall. She is at work on a new novel to be published by Virago in 1995. She lives in Northamptonshire.

MOY MCCRORY has published three collections of short stories. The latest *Those Sailing Ships of his Boyhood Dreams* was serialised by BBC radio. She has written one novel *The Fading Shrine* and is at work on a second. She was commissioned to write her first stage play last year, and is currently writing a second. She occasionally reviews, frequently tutors at London University, and lives in Salisbury.

SARAH SCHULMAN is the author of five novels: *Empathy, People in Trouble, After Delores, Girls, Visions and Everything* and *The Sophie Horowitz Story*. Her first non-fiction book, *My American History: Lesbian and Gay Life During the Reagan/Bush Years* will be published in 1994 and her new novel, *Rat Bohemia* will also appear in the USA, 1995.

LISA TUTTLE was born in Houston and spent most of her first three decades in Texas. After ten years in London she moved to the west coast of Scotland where she now lives with her family. Although she likes writing strange (horror/fantasy/SF/unclassifiable) fiction best, she has also worked as a journalist and written works of non-fiction, including *Encyclopedia of Feminism* (1986). She edited an anthology of original horror stories by women called *Skin of the Soul* and had three short story collections and four novels published, most recently *Lost Futures* in 1992.